A SINGLE ROSE

A SINGLE ROSE

Barbara Delinsky

This first world hardcover edition published 2009
in Great Britain and in the USA by
SEVERN HOUSE PUBLISHERS LTD of
9–15 High Street, Sutton, Surrey, England, SM1 1DF,
by arrangement with Harlequin Books.
First published 1987 in the USA in mass market format only.

British Library Cataloguing in Publication Data

Delinsky, Barbara.
  A single rose.
  1. Treasure hunt (Game)--Fiction. 2. Caribbean Area--
  Fiction. 3. Love stories.
  I. Title
  813.5'4-dc22

ISBN-13: 978-0-7278-6790-2   (cased)

To Jessica Z.,
whose imagination is an inspiration.

All Severn House titles are printed on acid-free paper.

Typeset by Palimpsest Book Production Ltd.,
Grangemouth, Stirlingshire, Scotland.
Printed and bound in Great Britain by
MPG Books Ltd., Bodmin, Cornwall.

VICTORIA LESSER TOOK A BREAK from the conversation to sit back and silently enjoy the two couples with her. They were a striking foursome. Neil Hersey, with his dark hair and close-cropped beard, was a perfect foil for his fair and petite wife, Deirdre, but the perfection of the match didn't stop at their looks. Deirdre's quick spirit complimented Neil's more studied approach to life. In the nineteen months of their marriage, they'd both grown personally and professionally.

As had the Rodenhisers. Though married a mere six months, they'd been together for nearly fifteen. Leah, with her glossy raven pageboy and bangs and the large round glasses perched on her nose, had found the ideal mate in Garrick, who gave her the confidence to live out her dreams. Garrick, sandy-haired, tall, and bearded like Neil, had finally tasted the richness of life that he'd previously assumed existed only in a scriptwriter's happy ending.

Glancing from one face to the next as the conversation flowed around her, Victoria congratulated herself on bringing the four together. It had been less of a brainstorm, of course, than her original matchmaking endeavors, but it was making for a lively and lovely evening.

Feeling momentarily superfluous, she let her gaze meander among the elegantly dressed patrons of the restaurant. She spotted several familiar faces on the far side of the room, and when her attention returned to her own party, she met Deirdre's eye. "Recognize them, Dee?"

Deirdre nodded and spoke in a hushed voice to her husband. "The Fitzpatricks and the Grants. They were at the lawn party Mother gave last fall."

Neil's wry grin was a flash of white cutting through his beard. His voice was low and smooth. "I'm not sure I remember the Fitzpatricks or the Grants, but I do remember that party. We were leaving Benji with a baby-sitter, and almost didn't get away. He was three months old and in one hell of a mood." He sent a lopsided grin across the table. "He takes after his mother in that respect."

Deirdre rolled her eyes. "Don't believe a word he says."

"Just tell me it gets better," Leah Rodenhiser begged. "You heard what Amanda gave us tonight."

Victoria, who had never had a child of her own and adored even the baby's wail, answered with the gentle voice of authority. "Of course it gets better. Amanda was just frightened. My apartment is strange and new to her. So is the baby-sitter. I left this number, but we haven't gotten a frantic call yet, have we?"

"I think you're about to get a frantic call from across the room," came a gravelly warning from Garrick. "They've spotted you, Victoria."

"Oh dear."

"Go on over," Deirdre urged softly. "If you don't, they'll come here. Spare us that joy. We'll talk babies until you get back."

Victoria, who knew all too well Deirdre's aversion to many of her mother's friends, shot her a chiding glance. But the glance quickly mellowed, and touched each of her guests in turn. "You don't mind?"

Leah grinned and answered for them all. "Go. We're traveling sub rosa."

"Sub rosa?"

"Incognito." Beneath the table she felt Garrick squeeze her hand. Once a well-known television star, he cherished his privacy. Basically shy herself, Leah protected it well.

"Are you sure you can manage without me?" Victoria quipped, standing when Neil drew out her chair. "Talk babies. I dare you." Her mischievous tone faded away as she headed off to greet her friends.

Four pairs of eyes watched her go, each pair as affectionate as the next. Victoria held a special place in their hearts, and they weren't about to talk babies when there were more immediate things to be said.

"She is a wonder," Leah sighed. "Little did I know what a gem I'd encountered when I ran into her that day in the library."

Neil was more facetious. "We didn't think she was such a gem when she stranded us on her island up in Maine. I don't think I've ever been as furious with anyone before."

"You were pretty furious with *me* before that day was out," Deirdre reminded him.

His grin grew devilish. "You asked for it. Lord, I wasn't prepared for you." He shifted his gaze to Leah and Garrick. "She was unbelievably bitchy. Had her leg in a cast and a mouth—"

Deirdre hissed him into silence, but couldn't resist reminiscing on her own. "It was just as well there weren't any neighbors. We'd have driven them crazy. We yelled at each other for days."

"While Leah and I were silent," Garrick said. "We were isolated in my cabin together, barely talking. I'm not sure which way is worse."

"Amazing how both worked out," Leah mused.

Deirdre nodded. "I'll second that."

"We owe Victoria one," Neil said.

"Two," Garrick amended.

Deirdre twirled the swizzle stick in her spritzer. "It's a tall order. The woman has just about everything she wants and needs."

Leah frowned. "There has to be something we can do in return for all she's given us."

"She needs a man."

Deirdre was quick to refute her husband's contention. "Come on, Neil. She has all the men she wants. And you know she'll never remarry. Arthur was the one and only love of her life."

Garrick exchanged a glance with Neil. "That doesn't mean we can't treat her to some fun."

Leah studied her husband. "I'm not sure I care for that mischievous gleam in your eye. Victoria is my friend. I won't have you—"

"She's my friend, too," he interrupted innocently. "Would I do anything to harm her?"

Neil was on Garrick's wavelength all the way. "The idea is to do something for her that she wouldn't dream up by herself."

"But she does just about everything she wants to," Deirdre pointed out. "She lives in luxury, dabbles in ballet, ceramics, the cello. She travels. She has the house in Southampton...." Her eyes brightened. "We could rent a yacht, hire a crew and put them at her disposal for a week. She'd be able to go off alone or invite friends along."

Garrick absently chafed his mustache with a finger. "Too conventional."

"How about a stint with Outward Bound?" Leah suggested. "There are groups formed specifically for women over forty."

Neil shot Garrick a look. "Not quite what I had in mind."

Deirdre had caught and correctly interpreted the look. "You have a one-track mind. Believe me, we'd be hard put to find a man with enough spunk for Victoria. Can you think of anyone suitable at Joyce?" Joyce Enterprises was Deirdre's family's corporation. Upon their marriage, Neil had taken it over and brought it from stagnation to productivity to expansion. Of the many new people he'd hired—or clients and associates of the company—Deirdre couldn't think of a single male who would be challenge enough for Victoria.

Neil's silence was ample show of agreement.

"It would be fun," Leah declared, "to turn the tables on Victoria."

"Someone good-looking," Deirdre said, warming to the idea.

Leah nodded. "And bright. We want a match here."

Neil rubbed his bearded jaw. "He'll have to be financially comfortable if he can afford to go in for adventure."

"Adventure," Garrick murmured. "That's the key."

Deirdre's brows lifted toward Neil. "Flash?" Flash Jensen was a neighbor of theirs in the central Connecticut suburb where they lived. A venture capitalist and a divorcé, he was always on the lookout for novel ways to spend his time.

Neil shook his head. "Flash is a little *too* much."

Leah chuckled. "We could always fix her up with one of Garrick's trapper friends. She'd die."

Garrick nodded, but he was considering another possibility. "There's a fellow I've met. One of my professors." Earlier he'd explained to the Herseys that he was working toward a Latin degree at Dartmouth. "Samson may well...fit the bill."

"Samson?" Leah echoed in mild puzzlement. She knew who he was, but nothing of what Garrick had told her in the past put the man forward as a viable candidate.

"He's a widower, and he's the right age."

Deirdre sat straighter. "Samson. From the name alone, I love him."

"That's because you've always had this thing about full heads of hair," Neil muttered in her ear. He'd never quite forgotten their earliest days together, when, among other things, she'd made fun of his widow's peak.

Deirdre hadn't forgotten either. As self-confident as Neil was, he had his sensitivities, and his hairline was one of them. "Forget hair," she whispered back. "Think strength. You have it even without the hair."

"You're putting your foot in deeper," he grumbled.

"I think you're right." Hastily she turned to Garrick, who'd been having a quiet discussion with Leah during the Herseys' private sparring. "Tell us about Samson."

Garrick was more than willing. "His name is Samson VanBaar. Leah thinks he's too conservative, but that's because she doesn't know him the way I do."

"He smokes a pipe," Leah informed them dryly.

"But that's all part of the image, love. Tweed jacket, pipe, tattered briefcase—he does it for effect. Tongue-in-cheek. A private joke."

"Weird private joke," was Leah's retort, but her tone had softened. "Do you really think he'd be right for Victoria?"

"If we're talking adventure, yes. He's good-looking and bright. He's independently wealthy. And he loves doing the unconventional." When Leah remained skeptical, he elaborated. "He's a private person, shy in some ways. He takes his little trips for his own pleasure, and they have nothing to do with the university. I had to coax him to talk, but once he got going, his stories were fascinating."

Deirdre sat forward, propping her chin in her hand. "We're listening."

"How does dog-sledding across the Yukon sound?"

"Challenging."

"How about a stint as a snake charmer in Bombay?"

"Not bad, if you're into snakes."

"Try living with the Wabians in Papua New Guinea."

"That does sound a little like Victoria," Leah had to admit. "When I first met her, she was boning up on the Maori of New Zealand."

Neil rubbed his hands together. "Okay. Let's see what we've got. A, the guy is okay in terms of age and marital status. B, he's good-looking and reasonably well-off. C, he's a respected member of the academic community." At the slight question in his voice, Garrick nodded. "And D, he's an adventurer." He took a slow breath. "So how do we go about arranging an adventure that Victoria could join him in?"

"I believe," Garrick said with a smug gleam in his eye, "it's already arranged. Samson VanBaar will be leaving next month for Colombia, from which point he'll sail across the Caribbean to Costa Rica in search of buried treasure."

"Buried treasure!"

"*Gold?*"

"He has a map," Garrick went on, his voice lower, almost secretive. "It's old and faded—"

"You've seen it?"

"You bet, and it looked authentic enough to me. Samson is convinced that it leads to a cache on the Costa Rican coast."

"It's so absurd, it's exciting!"

"Could be a wild goose chase. On the other hand—"

"Victoria would love it!"

"She very well might," Garrick concluded.

Neil was weighing the pros and cons. "Even if nothing comes of it in terms of a treasure, it'd certainly be a fun—how long?"

"I think he's allowed himself two weeks."

"Two weeks." Deirdre mulled it over. "Could be disastrous if they can't stand each other."

"She threw *us* together for two weeks, and we couldn't stand each other."

"It wasn't that we couldn't stand each other, Neil. We just had other things on our minds."

"We couldn't stand each other."

"Well, maybe at the beginning, but even then we couldn't keep our hands off each other."

Garrick coughed.

Leah rushed in to fill the momentary silence. "She threw us together for an *indefinite* period of time."

"Not that she planned it that way. She didn't count on mud season."

"That's beside the point. She sat by while I gave up my loft and put my furniture into storage. Then she sent me off to live in a cabin that had burned to the ground three months before. She knew I wouldn't have anywhere to go but your place, and those first few days were pretty tense...." Her words trailed off. Remembering the nights, she shot Garrick a shy glance and blushed.

Deirdre came to her aid. "There's one significant difference here, I believe. Victoria got us together in Maine; she got you two together in New Hampshire. Costa Rica—that's a little farther afield, and definitely foreign soil."

"It's a democratic country," Garrick pointed out, "and a peaceful one."

"Right next door to Nicaragua?" Leah asked in dismay, pushing her glasses higher on her nose as she turned to Neil. "Do you know anything about Costa Rica?"

"She *is* peaceful. Garrick's right about that. She's managed to stay out of her neighbors' turmoil. And she happens to be the wealthiest country in Central America."

"Then Victoria would be relatively safe?"

Garrick nodded.

"From Samson?" Deirdre asked. "Is he an honest sort of man?"

"Completely."

"Gentle?"

"Infinitely."

"Law abiding?"

"A Latin professor on tenure at one of the Ivies?" was Garrick's answer-by-way-of-a-question.

Neil stopped chewing on the inside of his cheek. "Is he, in any way, shape or manner, a lecher?"

"I've never heard any complaints," Garrick said. "Victoria can handle him. She's one together lady."

Having no argument there, Neil put the matter to an impromptu vote. "Are we in agreement that two weeks with Samson VanBaar won't kill her?"

Three heads nodded in unison.

"I'll speak with Samson and make the arrangements," Garrick offered. "I can't see that he'd have any objection to bringing one more person along on the trip, but we'd better not say anything to Victoria until I've checked it out."

"It'll be a surprise."

"She won't be able to refuse."

"She'll never know what hit her."

Garrick's lips twitched. "That'd be poetic justice, don't you think? After what she did to us—" His voice rose and he broke into his best show-stopping smile as the object of their discussion returned. "Hel-lo, Victoria!"

FIVE DAYS AFTER THAT DINNER in New York, Victoria received a bulky registered letter from New Hampshire. Opening it, she unfolded the first piece of paper she encountered.

"Dear Victoria," she read in Garrick's classic scrawl. "A simple thank you couldn't possibly convey our gratitude for all you've done. Hence, the enclosures. You'll find a round-trip ticket to Colombia, plus detailed instruction on where to go once you're there. You'll be taking part in a hunt for buried treasure led by one of my professors, a fascinating gentleman named Samson VanBaar. We happen to know you have no other plans for the last two weeks in July, and if you try to call us to weasel your way out, we won't be in. Samson is expecting you on the fourteenth. Have a wonderful time! All our love, Garrick and Leah and Deirdre and Neil."

Bemused, Victoria sank into the Louis XVI chair just inside the living-room arch. A treasure hunt? She set aside the plane tickets and read through the instructions and itinerary Garrick had seen fit to send.

New York to Miami to Barranquilla by plane. Accommodations in Barranquilla at El Prado, where Samson VanBaar would make contact. Brief drive from Barranquilla to Puerto Colombia. Puerto Colombia to Costa Rica—*Costa Rica*—by sail. Exploration of the Caribbean coast of Costa Rica as designated by Samson VanBaar's treasure map. Return by sail to Colombia and by plane to New York. Expect much sun, occasional rain. Dress accordingly.

The instructions joined the letter and tickets on her lap. She couldn't believe it! She'd known they had something up their sleeves when she'd returned to the table that night and seen smugness in their eyes.

They'd been sly; she had to hand it to them. They'd waited until the arrangements were made before presenting her with the fait accompli. Oh, yes, she could graciously refuse, but they knew she wouldn't. *She* knew she wouldn't. She'd never gone in search of buried treasure before, and though she certainly had no need for treasure, the prospect of the search was too much to resist!

Other things had been swirling around in those scheming minds of theirs as well. She knew because she'd been there herself. And because she'd been there, she knew it had something to do with Samson VanBaar. Were they actually fixing her up?

She'd sent Deirdre and Neil to the island in Maine after receiving separate, desperate calls begging for a place of solitude. She'd sent Leah to New Hampshire, to a cabin that didn't exist, knowing Leah would have no recourse but to seek out Garrick, her nearest neighbor on the mountain. What would Victoria find when she arrived in Colombia?

If Samson VanBaar was one of Garrick's professors, he had to be responsible. He might be wonderful. Or he might be forty years old and too young for her, or old and stuffy and too dry for her. One of Garrick's professors. A Latin professor. Definitely old and stuffy and dry. Perhaps simply the organizer of the expedition. In which case the Herseys and the Rodenhisers had someone else in mind. Someone else in the group?

There were many questions and far too few answers, but Victoria did know one thing. She had already blocked out the last two weeks in July for a treasure hunt. It was an opportunity, a challenge, an adventure. Regardless of her friends' wily intentions, she knew she could handle herself.

AS THAT DAY ZIPPED BY and the next began, Victoria couldn't help but think more and more about the trip. She had to admit that there was something irresistibly romantic about a sail through the Caribbean and a treasure hunt. Perhaps this Samson VanBaar would turn out to be a pirate at heart. Or perhaps one of the other group members would be the pirate.

That night, unable to shake a particularly whimsical thought, she settled in the chintz-covered chaise in the sitting area of her bedroom and put through a call to her niece.

"Hi there, Shaye!"

"Victoria?" Shaye Burke hadn't called Victoria "aunt" in years. Victoria was a dear friend with whom she'd weathered many a storm. "It's so good to hear your voice!"

"Yours, sweetheart, is sounding foreign. Do you have something against dialing the phone?"

Duly chastised, Shaye sank onto the tall stool by the kitchen phone and spoke with a fair amount of contrition. "I'm sorry, Victoria. Work's been hectic. By the time I get home my mind is addled."

"Did you just get in?"

"Mmm. We're in the process of installing a new system. It's time consuming, not to mention energy consuming." Shaye headed the computer department of a law firm in Philadelphia that specialized in corporate work. Victoria was familiar enough with such firms to know that computerization had become critical to their productivity.

"And the bulk of the responsibility is on your shoulders, I'd guess."

Shaye nodded, too tired to realize that Victoria couldn't see the gesture. "Not that I'm complaining. The new machines are incredible. Once we're fully on-line, we'll be able to do that much more that much more quickly."

"When will that be?"

"Hopefully by the end of next week. I'll have to work this weekend, but that's nothing new."

"Ahh, Shaye, where's your private life?"

"What's a private life?" Shaye returned with mock innocence.

Victoria saw nothing remotely amusing in the matter. "Private life is that time you spend away from work. It's critical, sweetheart. If you're not careful, you'll burn out before you're thirty."

"Then I'd better get on the stick. Four more months and I'll be there."

"I'm serious, Shaye. You work too hard and play too little."

Suddenly Shaye was serious, too. "I've played, Victoria. You know that better than anyone. I had six years of playing and the results were dreadful."

"You were a child then."

"I was twenty-three when I finally woke up. It was a pretty prolonged childhood, if you ask me."

"I'm not asking you, I'm telling you. What you did then was an irresponsible kind of playing. We've discussed this before, so I'm not breaking any new ground. When I use the word 'playing' now, I'm talking about something quite different. I'm talking about reading a good book, or going shopping just for the fun of it, or watching a fluff movie. I'm talking about spending time with friends."

Shaye knew what she was getting at. "I date."

"Oh yes. You've told me about those exciting times. Three hours talking shop with a lawyer from another firm. Another firm—that is daring. Of course, the fellow was nearly my age and probably arthritic."

Shaye chuckled. "We can't all reach fifty-three and be as agile as you."

"But you *can*. It's all in the mind. That lawyer's mind was no doubt ready for retirement five years ago. And your stockbroker friend doesn't sound much better. Does he give you good leads, at least?"

"It'd be illegal for me to act on an inside tip. You know that."

Victoria did know it. She also knew that her niece gave wide berth to anything vaguely questionable, let alone illegal. Shaye Burke had become a disgustingly respectable pillar of society. "Okay. Forget about stock tips. Let's talk fun. Do you have fun with him?"

"He's pleasant."

"So is the dentist. Have you been with anyone lately who's fun?"

"Uh-huh. Shannon."

"Shannon's your sister!" Victoria knew how close the two were; they'd always been so. Shaye, the elder by four years, felt personally responsible for Shannon. "She doesn't count. Who else?"

"Judy."

Victoria gave an inward groan. Judy Webber was a lawyer in Shaye's firm. The two women had become friends. If occasional weekend barbecues with Judy, her husband and their two teenaged daughters comprised Shaye's attempts at relaxation, she was in pretty bad shape.

"How is Judy?" Victoria asked politely.

"Fine. She and Bob are heading for Nova Scotia next week. She's looking forward to it."

"That does sound nice. In fact, that's one of the reasons I called."

"To hear about Judy and Bob and Nova Scotia?"

"To talk to you about *your* vacation plans. I need two weeks of your time, sweetheart. The last two weeks in July."

"Two weeks? Victoria, I can't take off in July."

"Why not?"

"Because I'm scheduled for vacation in August."

"Schedules can be changed."

"But I've already made reservations."

"Where?"

"In the Berkshires. I've rented a cottage."

"Alone?"

"Of course alone. How else will I manage to do the reading and shopping and whatever else you claim I've been missing?"

"Knowing the way you've worked yourself to the bone, you'll probably spend the two weeks sleeping."

"And what more peaceful a place to sleep than in the country?"

"Sleeping is boring. You don't accomplish anything when you sleep."

"We're not all like you," Shaye pointed out gently. "You may be able to get by on five hours of sleep a night, but I need eight."

"And you don't usually get them because you work every night, then get up with the sun the next day to return to the office."

Shaye didn't even try to refute her aunt's claim. All she could do was rationalize. "I have six people under me—six people I'm responsible for. The hours are worth it because the results are good. I take pride in my work. And I'm paid well for my time."

"You must be building up quite some kitty in the bank, because I don't see you spending much of that money on yourself."

"I do. I live well."

"You're about to live better," Victoria stated firmly. "Two weeks in July. As my companion."

Shaye laughed. "Your companion? That's a new one."

"This trip is."

"What trip?"

"We're going to Colombia, you and I, and then on to Costa Rica."

"You aren't serious."

"Very. We're going on a treasure hunt."

Shaye stared at the receiver before returning it to her ear. "Want to run that by me again?"

"A treasure hunt, Shaye. We'll fly to Barranquilla, spend the night in a luxury hotel, drive to Puerto Colombia and then sail in style across the Caribbean. You can do all the sleeping you want on the boat. By the time we reach Costa Rica you'll be refreshed and ready to dig for pirates' gold."

Shaye made no attempt to muffle her moan. "Oh, Victoria, where did you dream this one up?"

"I didn't dream it up. It was handed to me on a silver platter. The expedition is being led by a friend of a friend, a professor from Dartmouth who even has a map."

"Pirates' gold?" Shaye echoed skeptically.

Victoria waved a negligent hand in the air. "Well, I don't actually know what the treasure consists of, but it sounds like a fun time, don't you think?"

"I think it sounds—"

"Absurd. I knew you would, but believe me, sweetheart, this is a guaranteed adventure."

"For you. But why *me*?"

"Because I need you along for protection."

"Come again?"

"I need you for protection."

Shaye's laugh was even fuller this time. "The day you need protection will be the day they put you in the ground, and even then, I suspect they'll be preparing for outrageous happenings at the pearly gates. Try another one."

Anticipating resistance, Victoria had thought of every possible argument. This one was her most powerful, so she repeated it a third time, adding a note of desperation to her voice. "I need your protection, Shaye. This trip was arranged for me by some friends, and I'm sure they have mischief in mind."

"And you'd drag me along to suffer their mischief? No way, Victoria. I'm not in the market for mischief."

"They're trying to fix me up. I know they are. Their hearts are in the right place, but I don't need fixing up. I don't want it." She lowered her voice. "You, of all people, ought to understand."

Shaye understood all too well. Closing her eyes, she tried to recall the many times people had tried—the many times

Victoria herself had tried—to fix her up with men who were sure to be the answer to her prayers. What they failed to realize was that Shaye's prayers were different from most other people's.

"All I'm asking," Victoria went on in the same deliberately urgent tone, "is that you act as a buffer. If I have you with me, I won't be quite so available to some aging lothario."

"What if they're fixing you up with a younger guy? It's done all the time."

Then he's all yours, sweetheart. "No. My friends wouldn't do that. At least," she added after sincere pause, "I don't think they would."

Shaye began, one by one, to remove the pins that had held her thick auburn hair in a twist since dawn. "I can't believe you're asking this of me," she said.

Victoria wasn't about to be touched by the weariness in her voice. "Have I ever asked much else?"

"No."

"And think of what you'll be getting out of the trip yourself. A luxurious sail through the Caribbean. Plenty of sun and clean air. We can spend a couple of extra days in Barranquilla if you want."

"Victoria, I don't even know if I can arrange for those two weeks, let alone a couple of extra days."

"You can arrange it. I have faith."

"You always have faith. That's the trouble. Now your faith is directed at some pirate stash. For years and years people have been digging for pirate treasure. Do you honestly believe anything's left to be found?"

"The point of the trip isn't the treasure, it's the hunt. And for you it will be the rest and the sun and—"

"The clean air. I know."

"Then you'll come?"

"I don't know if I can."

"You have to. I've already made the arrangements." It was a little white lie, but Victoria felt it was justified. She'd simply call Samson VanBaar and tell him one more person would be joining them. What was another person? Shaye ate like a bird, and if there was a shortage of sleeping space, Victoria herself would scrunch up on the floor.

"You're forcing me into this," Shaye accused, but her voice held an inkling of surrender.

"That's right."

"If I say no, you'll probably call the senior partner of my firm first thing tomorrow."

"I hadn't thought of that, but it's not a bad idea."

Shaye screwed up her face. "Isn't there *anyone* else you can bring along in my place?"

"No one I'd rather be with."

"That's emotional blackmail."

"So be it."

"Oh, Victoria . . ."

"Is that a yes?"

For several minutes, Shaye said nothing. She didn't want to traipse off in search of treasure. She didn't want to take two weeks in July, rather than the two weeks she'd planned on in August. She didn't want to have to spend her vacation acting as a buffer, when so much of her time at work was spent doing that.

But Victoria was near and dear to her. Victoria had stood by her, compassionate and forgiving when she'd nearly made a mess of her life. Victoria understood her, as precious few others did.

"Are we on?" came the gentle voice from New York.

From Philadelphia came a sigh, then a soft-spoken, if resigned, "We're on."

Later that night, as Shaye worked a brush through the thick fall of her hair, she realized that she'd given in for two basic reasons. The first was the she adored Victoria. Time spent with her never failed to be uplifting.

The second was that, in spite of all she might say to the contrary, the thought of spending two weeks in a rented cottage in the Berkshires had a vague air of loneliness to it.

VICTORIA, MEANWHILE, basked in her triumph without the slightest twinge of guilt. Shaye needed rest, and she'd get it. She needed a change of scenery, and she'd get that too. Adventure was built into the itinerary, and along the way if a man materialized who could make her niece laugh the way she'd done once upon a time, so much the better.

A spunky doctoral candidate would do the trick. Or a fun-loving assistant professor. Samson VanBaar had to be bringing a few interesting people along on the trip, didn't he?

She glanced at the temple clock atop a nearby chest. Was ten too late to call? Definitely not. One could learn a lot about a man by phoning him at night.

Without another thought, she contacted information for Hanover, New Hampshire, then punched out his home number. The phone rang twice before a rather bland, not terribly young female voice came on the line. "Hello," it said. "You have reached the residence of Samson VanBaar. The professor is not in at the moment. If you'd care to leave a message, he will be glad to return your call. Please wait for the sound of the tone."

Victoria thought quickly as she waited. Nothing learned here; the man could be asleep or he could be out. But perhaps it was for the best that she was dealing with a machine. She could leave her message without giving him a chance to refuse her request on the spot.

The tone sounded.

"This is Victoria Lesser calling from New York. Garrick Rodenhiser has arranged for me to join your expedition to

Costa Rica, but there has been a minor change in my plans. My niece, Shaye Burke, will be accompanying me. She is twenty-nine, attractive, intelligent and hardworking. I'll personally arrange for her flight to and from Colombia, and, of course, I'll pay all additional costs. Assuming you have no problem with this plan, Shaye and I will see you in Barranquilla on the fourteenth of July."

Pleased with herself, she hung up the phone.

Four days later, she received a cryptic note typed on a plain postcard. The postmark read, "Hanover, NH," and the note read, very simply, "Received your message and have made appropriate arrangements. Until the fourteenth—VanBaar."

Though it held no clue to the man himself, at least he hadn't banned Shaye from the trip, and for that she was grateful. Shaye had called the night before to say she'd managed to clear the two weeks with her firm, and Victoria had already contacted both the Costa Rican Embassy in New York regarding visas and her travel agent regarding a second set of airline tickets.

They were going on a treasure hunt. No matter what resulted in the realm of romance, Victoria was sure of one thing: come hell or high water, she and Shaye were going to have a time to remember.

2

THE FOURTEENTH OF JULY was not one of Shaye's better days. Having worked late at the office the night before to clear her desk, then rushing home to pack for the trip, she'd gotten only four hours' sleep before rising to shower, dress and catch an early train into New York to meet Victoria. Their plane was forty-five minutes late leaving Kennedy and the flight was a turbulent one, though Shaye suspected that a certain amount of the turbulence she experienced was internal. She had a headache and her stomach wouldn't settle. It didn't help that they nearly missed their transfer in Miami, and when they finally landed in Barranquilla, their luggage took forever to appear. She was cursing the Colombian heat by the time they reached their hotel, and after waiting an additional uncomfortable hour for their room to be ready, she discovered that she'd gotten her period.

"Why me?" she moaned softly as she curled into a chair.

Victoria came to the rescue with aspirin and water. "Here, sweetheart. Swallow these down, then take a nap. You'll feel better after you've had some sleep."

Not about to argue, when all she wanted was an escape from her misery, Shaye dutifully swallowed the aspirin, then undressed, sponged off the heat of the trip, drew back the covers of one of the two double beds in the room and slid between the sheets. She was asleep within minutes.

It was evening when a gentle touch on her shoulder awakened her. Momentarily disoriented, she peered around the room, then up at Victoria.

"You missed the zoo."

"Huh?"

"And you didn't even know I'd gone. Shame on you. But I'm back, and I thought I'd get a bite to eat. Want anything?"

Shaye began to struggle up, but Victoria easily pressed her back to the bed.

"No, no, sweetheart. I'll bring it here. You need rest far more than you need to sit in a restaurant."

Shaye was finally getting her bearings. "But . . . your professor. Aren't we supposed to meet him?"

Settling on the edge of the bed, Victoria shook her head. "He sent a message saying he'll be tied up stocking the boat for a good part of the night. We're to meet him there tomorrow morning at nine."

"Where's there?"

"A small marina in Puerto Colombia, about fifteen miles east of here. The boat is called the *Golden Echo*."

"The *Golden Echo*. Appropriate."

Victoria gave an impish grin. "I thought so, too. Pirates' gold. Echoes of the past. It's probably just a coincidence, since I assume the boat is rented."

"Don't assume it. If VanBaar does this sort of thing often, he could well own the boat." She hesitated, then ventured cautiously, "He does do this sort of thing often, doesn't he?"

"I really don't know."

"How large is the boat?"

"I don't know that either."

"How large is our group?"

Victoria raised both brows, pressed her lips together in a sheepish kind of way and shrugged.

"Victoria," Shaye wailed, fully awake now and wishing she weren't, "don't you ask questions before you jump into things?"

"What do I need to ask? I know that Samson VanBaar is Garrick's friend, and I trust Garrick."

"You dragged me along because you *didn't* trust him."

"I didn't trust that he wouldn't try to foist me off on some unsuspecting man, but that's a lesser issue here. The greater issue is the trip itself. Garrick would never pull any punches in the overall scheme of things."

Shaye tugged at a hairpin that was digging into her scalp. "Exactly what *do* you know about this trip?"

"Just what I've told you."

"Which is precious little."

"Come on, sweetheart. The details will come. They'll unfold like a lovely surprise."

"I hate surprises."

"Mmm. You like to know what's happening before it happens. That's the computerized you." Her gaze dropped briefly to the tiny mark at the top of Shaye's breast, a small shadow beneath the lace edging of her bra. "But there's another side, Shaye, and this trip's going to bring it out. You'll learn to accept it and control it. It's really not such a bad thing when taken in moderation."

"Victoria . . ."

"Look at it this way. You're with me. I'll be your protector, just as you'll be mine."

"How can you protect me from something you can't anticipate?"

"Oh, I can anticipate." She tipped up her head and fixed a dreamy gaze on the wall. "I'm anticipating that boat. It'll be a beauty. Long and sleek, with polished brass fittings and crisp white sails. We'll have a lovely stateroom to share. The food will be superb, the martinis nice and dry . . ."

"You hope."

"And why not? Look around. I wouldn't exactly call this room a hovel."

"No, but it could well be the equivalent of a last meal for the condemned."

Victoria clucked her tongue. "Such pessimism in one so young."

Shaye shifted onto her side. She was achy all over. "Right about now, I feel ninety years old."

"When you're ninety, you won't have to worry about monthly cramps. When you're fifty, for that matter." She grinned. "I rather like my age."

"What's not to like about sixteen?"

"Now, now, do I sound that irresponsible?"

"Carefree may be a better word, or starry-eyed, or naive. Victoria, for all you know the *Golden Echo* may be a leaky tub and Samson VanBaar a blundering idiot."

Victoria schooled her expression to one of total maturity. "I've thought a lot about that. Samson won't be an idiot. Maybe an absentminded professor, or a man bent on living out his childhood dreams." She took a quick breath. "He could be fun."

"He could be impossible."

"But there will be others aboard."

"Mmm. A bunch of his students, all around twenty and so full of themselves that they'll be obnoxious."

"You were pretty full of yourself at that age," she reminded her niece, smoothing a stray wisp of hair from Shaye's pale cheek.

"And obnoxious."

"You didn't think so at the time."

"Neither will they."

But Victoria's eyes had grown thoughtful again. "I don't think there'll be many students. Garrick wouldn't have signed me on as a dorm mother. No, I'd guess that we'll be encountering adults, people very much like us looking for a break from routine."

"Since when do you have a routine you need a break from?"

"Not me. You. You need the break. I don't need anything, but my friends wanted to give me a good time, and that's exactly what I intend to have." She pushed herself gracefully from the bed. "Starting now. I'm famished. What'll it be—a doggie bag from the restaurant or room service later?"

Shaye tucked up her knees and closed her eyes. "Sleep. Tomorrow will be soon enough for superb food and nice dry martinis."

THE TWO WOMEN HAD NO TROUBLE finding the *Golden Echo* the next morning. She was berthed at the end of the pier and very definitely stood apart from the other craft they'd passed.

"Oh Lord," Shaye muttered.

Victoria was as wide-eyed as her niece. "Maybe we have the wrong one."

"The name board says *Golden Echo*."

"Maybe I got the name wrong."

"Maybe you got the trip wrong."

They stood with their elbows linked and their heads close together as, eyes transfixed on the boat before them, they whispered back and forth.

"She isn't exactly a tub," Victoria offered meekly.

"She's a pirate ship—"

"In miniature."

"Looks like she's been through one too many battles. Or one too few. She should have sunk long ago."

"Maybe not," Victoria argued, desperately searching for something positive to say. "She looks sturdy enough."

"Like a white elephant."

"But she's clean."

"Mmm. The chipped paint's been neatly scraped away. Lord, I don't believe I've seen anything as boxy since the Tall Ships passed through during the Bicentennial."

"They were impressive."

"*They* were."

"So's this—"

"If you close your eyes and pretend you're living in the eighteenth century."

Victoria didn't close her eyes, but she was squinting hard. "You have to admit that she has a certain . . . character."

"Mmm. Decrepit."

"She takes three sails. That should be pretty."

Her enthusiasm was lost on Shaye, who was eyeing in dismay the ragged bundles of canvas lashed to the rigging. "Three crisp . . . white . . . sails."

"Okay, they may not be crisp and white. What does it matter, if they're strong?"

"Are they?"

"If Samson VanBaar is any kind of friend to Garrick—and if Garrick is any kind of friend to me—they are."

Shaye moaned. "And to think that I could have been in the Berkshires, lazing around without a care in the world."

"You'll be able to laze around here."

"I don't see any deck chairs."

"But it's a nice broad deck."

"It looks splintery."

"So we'll lie on towels."

"Did you bring some?"

"Of course not. They'll have towels aboard."

"Like they have polished brass fittings?" Shaye sighed. "Well, you were right in a way."

"What way was that?" Victoria asked, at a momentary loss.

"We are going in style. Of course, it's not exactly *our* style—for that matter, I'm not sure whose style it is." Her voice hardened. "You may be crazy enough to give it a try, but I'm not."

She started to pivot away, intending to take the first cab back to Barranquilla, but Victoria clamped her elbow tighter and dragged her forward. "Excuse me," she was calling, shading her eyes from the sun with her free hand. "We're looking for Samson VanBaar."

Keeping step with her aunt through no will of her own, Shaye forced herself to focus on the figure that had just emerged from the bowels of the boat. "It gets worse," she moaned, then whispered a hoarse, "What *is* he?"

"I'm VanBaar," came the returning call. "Mrs. Lesser, Miss Burke?" With a sweep of his arm, he motioned them forward. "We've been expecting you."

Nothing they'd imagined had prepared either Shaye or Victoria for Samson VanBaar. In his mid to late fifties, he was remarkably tall and solid. His well-trimmed salt-and-pepper hair, very possibly combed in a dignified manner short days before, tumbled carelessly around his head, forming a reckless frame for a face that was faintly sunburned, though inarguably sweet.

What was arguable was his costume, and it could only be called that. He wore a billowy white shirt tucked into a pair of narrow black pants, which were tucked into knee-high leather boots. A wide black belt slanted low across his hips, and if it lacked the scabbard for a dagger or a sword, the effect was the same.

"He forgot the eye patch," Shaye warbled hysterically.

"Shh! He's darling!" Victoria whispered under her breath. Smiling broadly—and never once releasing Shaye, who, she knew, would head in the opposite direction given the first opportunity—she started up the gangplank. At the top, she

put her free hand in the one Samson offered and stepped onto
the deck. "It's a delight to meet you at last, Professor Van-
Baar. I'm Victoria Lesser, and this is my niece, Shaye Burke."

Shaye was too busy silently cursing her relationship with
Victoria to say much of anything, but she managed a feeble
smile in return for the open one the professor gave her.

"Welcome to the *Golden Echo*," he said, quietly now that
they were close. "I trust you had no problem finding us."

"No, no," Victoria answered brightly. "None at all." She
made a grand visual sweep of the boat, trying to see as little
as possible while still conveying her point. "This is charming!"

Shaye nearly choked. When Victoria gave a tight, warning squeeze to her elbow before abruptly releasing it, she
tipped back her head, closed her eyes and drew in an exaggerated lungful of Caribbean air. It was certainly better than
having to look at the boat, and though Samson VanBaar was
attractive enough, the insides of her eyelids were more re-
assuring than his getup.

"I felt that the *Golden Echo* would be more in keeping with
the spirit of this trip than a modern yacht would be," he explained. "She's a little on the aged side, but I've been told she's
trusty."

Shaye opened one eye. "You haven't sailed her yet?"

Almost imperceptibly he ducked his head, but the tiny
movement was enough to suggest guilt. "I've sailed ones like
her, but I just flew in yesterday myself, and the bulk of my
time between then and now had been spent buying supplies.
I hope you understood why I couldn't properly welcome you
in Barranquilla last night."

"Of course," Victoria reassured him gently. "It worked out
just as well, actually. We were both tired after the flight."

"You slept well?"

"Very well."

"Good." He ran a forefinger along the corner of his mouth, as though unsure of what to say next. Then his eyes brightened. "Your bags." He quickly spotted them on the pier. "Let me bring them aboard, then I'll give you the Cook's tour."

He'd no sooner descended the gangplank when Shaye whirled on Victoria. "The Cook's tour?" she whispered wildly. "Is he the cook or are we?"

"Don't fret," Victoria whispered back with confidence, "there's a cook."

"Like there's a lovely stateroom for us to share? Do you have any idea what's down there?"

"Nope. That's what the Cook's tour is for."

"Aren't you worried?"

"Of course not. This is an adventure."

"The boat is a wreck!"

"She's trusty."

"So says the professor who's staging Halloween three months early."

Victoria's eyes followed Samson's progress. "And I thought he'd be stuffy. He's precious!"

"Good. Since you like him so well, you won't need my protection after all. I'll just take my bag and head back—"

"You will not! You're staying!"

"Victoria, there'll be lots of other people..." The words died on her lips. Her head remained still while her eyes moved from one end of the empty deck to the other. She listened. "Where are they? It's too quiet. We were ten minutes late, ourselves. Where are the others?"

Victoria was asking herself the same question. Her plan was contingent on there being other treasure seekers, specifically of the young and good-looking male variety. True, in terms of rest alone, the trip would be good for Shaye, and Victoria always enjoyed her niece's company. But matching her up with a man—it had worked so well with Deirdre, then Leah . . . Where *were* the men?

Concealing her concern behind a gracious smile, she turned to VanBaar, who had rejoined them with a suitcase in either hand. "We don't expect you wait on us. Please. Just tell us what to do." She reached for her bag, but Samson drew it out of her reach.

"Chivalry is a dying art. You'll have plenty to do as time goes on, but for now, I think I can manage two bags."

Chivalry? Shaye thought, amused. *Plenty to do?* she thought, appalled.

Victoria was thinking about the good-looking young men she didn't see. "Is this standard service given to all the members of your group?" she ventured, half teasing, half chiding, and subtly fishing for information.

"No, ma'am. We men fend for ourselves. You and your niece are the only women along."

Swell, Shaye groused silently, *just swell*.

Victoria couldn't have been more delighted. "How many others are there, Professor VanBaar?"

He blushed. "Samson, please."

She smiled. "Samson, then. How many of us will there be in all?"

"Four."

"Four?" the women echoed in unison.

"That's right." Setting the bags by his booted feet, he scratched the back of his head. "Didn't Garrick explain the situation?"

Victoria gave a delicate little cough. "I'm afraid he didn't go quite that far."

"That was negligent of him," Samson said, but he didn't seem upset, and Victoria saw a tiny twinkle in his eye. "Let me explain. Originally there were to be just two of us, myself and an old college buddy with whom I often travel in the summer. When Garrick called me about your joining us, I saw no problem. Unfortunately, my friend had to cancel at the last minute, so I hoodwinked my nephew into taking up the slack." He stole a glance at Shaye's dismayed expression. "It takes two to comfortably man the boat, and since I didn't know whether either of you were sailors—"

"We're not," Shaye burst out. "I don't know about my aunt, but I get seasick."

"Ignore her, Samson. She's only teasing."

"*Violently* seasick."

"Not to worry," Samson assured her in the same kind tone that made it hard to hold a grudge. "I have medicine for seasickness, though I doubt you'll need it. We shouldn't run into heavy seas."

At that moment, Shaye would have paid a pirate's ransom to be by her lonesome in the Berkshires. A foursome—Victoria and Samson, Samson's nephew and her. It was too cozy, too convenient. Suddenly something smacked of a setup. Could Samson have done it? Or Garrick? Or . . . She skewered her aunt with an accusatory glare.

Victoria had her eyes glued to Samson. "I'm sure we'll be fine." She took a deep breath and straightened her shoulders. "Now then, I believe you said something about a tour?"

NOAH VANBAAR WAS nearly as disgusted as Shaye. Arms crossed over his chest and one knee bent up as he lounged on a hardwood bench within earshot of the three above, he struggled in vain to contain his frustration. He'd had other plans for his summer vacation, but when his uncle had called, claiming that Barney was sick and there was no one else who could help him sail, he'd been indulgent.

Samson and he were the only two surviving members of the VanBaar family, but even if sentimentality hadn't been a factor, Noah was fond enough of his uncle to take pity. He knew how much Samson looked forward to his little jaunts. He also knew that Samson was an expert sailor and more than capable of handling the boat himself, but that for safety's sake he needed another pair of hands along. If Noah's refusal meant that Samson had to cancel his trip, there was no real choice to be made.

Naturally, his uncle had waited until last night to inform him that they wouldn't be sailing alone. Naturally, he had waited until this morning to inform him that the pair joining them would be female.

Noah didn't want one woman along, much less two. Not that he had anything against women in general, but on this trip, they would be in the way. He'd planned to relax, to take a break from the tension that was part and parcel of his work. He'd planned to have one of the two cabins on the boat to himself, to sleep to his heart's content, to dress as he pleased, shave when and if he pleased, swim in the buff, and, in short, let it all hang out.

The presence of women didn't figure into his personal game plan. They were bound to screw things up. A widow and her niece. Charming. Samson was already carrying their bags. If they thought *he* was going to wait on them, they had another think coming!

Actually, he mused, the aunt didn't sound so bad. She had a pleasant voice, sounded lively without being obnoxious, and to her further credit, had protested Samson's playing bellboy. He wondered what she looked like and whether Samson would be enthralled. He hoped not, because then he'd be stuck with the niece, who sounded far less lively and more obnoxious than her aunt.

It was obvious that the niece wasn't thrilled with the looks of the sloop. What had she expected? The *Brittania*? If so, he decided as his eyes skimmed the gloomy interior of the

Golden Echo, she was in for an even ruder awakening than she'd already had.

Not that the boat bothered him; he'd sailed in far worse. This time around, though, he could have asked for more space. This time around he'd have preferred the *Brittania*, himself. At least then he'd have been able to steer clear of the women.

Though he didn't move an inch, he grew instinctively alert when he heard footsteps approaching the gangway. Samson was in the lead, his booted feet appearing several seconds before the two suitcases. "The *Golden Echo* was refurbished ten years ago," he was saying, his voice growing louder as his head came into view. "The galley is quite modern and the cabins comfortable—ah, Noah, right where I left you." Stepping aside, he set down the bags to give an assisting hand to each of the women in turn.

Noah didn't have to marvel at his uncle's style. Though a bit eccentric at times, Samson was a gentleman through and through, which was fine as long as he didn't expect the same standard from his nephew. Noah spent his working life straddling the lines between gentleman, diplomat and czar; he intended to spend his vacation answering to no one but himself.

"Noah, I'd like you to meet Victoria Lesser," Samson said. He knew better than to ask his nephew to rise. Noah was intimidating enough when seated; standing he was formidable. Given the dark mood he was in at the moment, intimidation was the lesser of the evils.

Noah nodded toward Victoria, careful to conceal the slight surprise he felt. Victoria had not only sounded lively, she looked lively. What had Samson said—that she was in her early fifties? She didn't look a day over forty. She wore a bright yellow, oversize shirt, a pair of white slacks with the cuffs rolled to mid-calf, and sneakers, and her features were every bit as youthful. Her hair was an attractive walnut shade and thick, loosely arranged into a high, short ponytail that left gentle wisps to frame the delicate structure of her face. Her skin was flawless, firm-toned and lightly made up, if at all. Her eyes twinkled, and her smile was genuine.

"It's a pleasure to meet you, Noah," she said every bit as sincerely. "Thank you for letting us join you on this trip. I've done many things in my day, but I've never been on a treasure hunt before. It sounds as though it'll be fun."

Lured by the subtle melody of her voice, Noah almost believed her. Then he shifted his gaze to the young woman who'd followed her down the steps and took back the thought.

"Shaye Burke," Samson was saying by way of introduction, "Noah VanBaar."

Again Noah nodded his head, this time a trifle more stiffly. Shaye Burke was a looker; he had to give her that. Slightly taller than her aunt, she was every bit as slender. Her white jeans were pencil thin, her blousy, peach-colored T-shirt rolled at the sleeves and knotted chicly at the waist. Her skin, too, was flawless, but it was pale; she'd skillfully applied makeup to cover shadows beneath her eyes and add faint color to her cheeks.

Any similarities to her aunt had already ended. Shaye's deep auburn hair was anchored at the nape of her neck in a sedate twist from which not a strand escaped. The younger woman's lips were set, her nose marked with tension, and the eyes that met his held a shadow of rebellion.

She didn't want to be here. It was written all over her face. Adding that to the comments he'd overheard earlier, he begrudged her presence more than ever. If Shaye Burke did anything to spoil his uncle's adventure, he vowed, he would personally even the score.

Samson, who'd sensed the instant animosity between Noah and Shaye, spoke up quickly. "If you ladies will come this way, I'll show you to your cabin. Once we've deposited your things there, we can walk around more freely."

Short of turning and fleeing, Shaye had no choice but to follow Victoria, who followed Samson through the narrow passageway. Her shoulders were ramrod straight, held that way by the force of a certain man's gaze piercing her back.

Noah. Noah and Samson. The VanBaar family, she decided, had a thing about biblical names. But her image of *that* Noah was one of kindness; *this* Noah struck her as being quite different. Sitting in the shadows as he'd been, she hadn't been able to see much beyond gloom and a glower. She knew one thing, though: She hadn't expected to have to protect her aunt, but if Noah VanBaar so much as dared do anything to dampen Victoria's spirits, he'd have to answer to her.

SAMSON LED VICTORIA AND SHAYE to the cabin they'd be sharing, then backtracked to show them the salon, the galley and the captain's quarters in turn. Noah was nowhere in sight during the backtracking, and Shaye was grateful for that. There was precious little else to be grateful for.

"We do have our own bathroom," Victoria pointed out when they'd returned to their cabin to unpack. She lowered herself to Shaye's side of the double bed that occupied three quarters of the small cabin's space. "I know that it's not quite what we expected, but if we clear our minds of those other expectations, we'll do fine."

Shaye's lips twisted wryly. "Grin and bear it?"

"Make the most of it." She jabbed at the bedding with a delicate fist. "The mattress feels solid enough." Her eye roamed the trapezoid-shaped room. "And we could have been stuck with a V-berth."

"This bed is bolted to the wall. I thought Samson said it'd be a calm trip."

"This one will be, but we have no idea what other waters the *Golden Echo* has sailed."

"If only she were somewhere else—without us."

"Shaye . . ."

"And where do we go to relax?"

"The salon."

"For privacy?" She was thinking of the dagger-edged gaze that had followed her earlier, and wasn't sure whether she'd be able to endure it as a constant.

Victoria's mind was still on the salon. "There are comfortable chairs, a sofa—"

"And a distinctly musty smell."

"That's the smell of the sea. It adds atmosphere."

Shaye snorted. "That kind of atmosphere I can do without." She knew she was being unfair; after all, the cottage she'd booked in the Berkshires very probably had its own musty smell, and she normally wasn't that fussy. But her bad mood seemed to feed on itself and on every tiny fault she could find with the boat.

"Come on, sweetheart," Victoria coaxed as she rose to open her suitcase. "We'll have fun. I promise."

Shaye's discouraged gaze wandered around the cabin, finally alighting on the row of evenly spaced, slit-like windows. "At least there are portholes. Clever, actually. They're built into the carving of the hull. I didn't notice them from the dock."

"And they're open. The air's circulating. And it's relatively bright."

"All the better to see the simplicity of the decor," Shaye added tongue-in-cheek. She watched her aunt unpack in silence for several minutes before tipping her head to the side and venturing a wary, "Victoria?"

"Uh-huh?"

"How much did you really know about all this?"

Victoria stacked several pairs of shorts in a pile, then straightened. "About all what?"

"This trip."

"Haven't we discussed this before?"

"But something's beginning to smell."

"I told you," Victoria responded innocently. "It's the sea."

"Not smell as in brine. Smell as in rat. Did you have any idea at all that there'd be just four of us?"

"Of course not."

"It never occurred to you that Samson would be 'precious' and that I'd be left with his nephew?"

Victoria gave a negligent shrug and set the shorts in the nearby locker. "You heard what Samson said. Noah's joining us was a last-minute decision. I mentioned this trip to you nearly a month ago."

But Shaye remained skeptical. "Samson didn't say exactly how 'last-minute' the decision was. Are you sure you're not trying to pair me up with Noah?"

"Would I do that—"

"She asks a little too innocently. You did it with Deirdre Joyce."

"I thought you approved."

"In that case I did—do. Neil Hersey is a wonderful man." Shaye had never forgotten that it was Neil, with his legal ability and compassion, who had come to the rescue when Shannon had been arrested.

Victoria was grateful that Shaye knew nothing of her role in bringing Garrick and Leah together. The less credence given the word *matchmaker*, the better, she decided. "Noah VanBaar may be every bit as wonderful."

Shaye coughed comically. "Try again."

"He may be!"

"Then you did do it on purpose?"

Victoria felt only a smidgen of guilt as she propped her hands on her hips in a stance of exasperation. "Really, Shaye. How could I have done it on purpose when I had no idea Noah would be along?"

"Then you intended to fix me up with Samson's old-fart friend?"

"I did not! I truly, truly expected that we'd be only two more members of a larger group."

Sensing a certain truth to that part of Victoria's story at least, Shaye sighed. "If only there *were* a larger group—"

"So you could fade into the woodwork? I wouldn't have let you do that even if there were fifty others on board this boat." She lifted a pair of slacks and nonchalantly shook them out. "What did you think of Noah, by the way?"

"I thought he was rude, by the way. He could have stood up when we were introduced. He could have said something. Do you realize the man didn't utter a single word?"

"Neither did you at that point."

"That's because I chose silence over saying something unpleasant."

"Maybe that's what he was doing. Maybe he's as tired as you are. Maybe he, too, had other plans before Samson called him."

"I wish he'd stuck to his guns."

"Like you did?"

Bowing her head, Shaye pressed the throbbing spot between her eyes. "I gave in because you're my aunt and my friend and because I love you."

Draping an arm around Shaye's shoulders, Victoria hugged her close. "You know how much that means to me, sweetheart. And it may be that Noah feels the same about Samson. Cheer up. He won't be so bad. How can he be, with an uncle like that?"

WHEN VICTORIA LEFT to go on deck, Shaye stayed behind to unpack. But there was only so much unpacking to do, and only so much to look at within the close cabin walls. She realized she was stalling, and that annoyed her, then hardened her. If Noah VanBaar thought he could cower her with his dark and brooding looks, he was in for a surprise.

Emboldened, she made her way topside to find Samson drawing up the gangplank. A powerboat hovered at the bow of the *Golden Echo*, prepared to tow her clear of the pier. At Samson's call, Noah cast off the lines, the powerboat accelerated and they were off.

When the other three gathered at the bow, Shaye took refuge at the stern. Mounting the few steps to the ancient version of a cockpit, she bypassed the large wooden wheel to rest against the transom and watch the shore slowly but steadily recede.

It was actually a fine day for a sail, she had to admit. The breeze feathered her face, cooling what might otherwise have been heated rays of the sun. But she felt a wistfulness as her gaze encompassed more and more of the Colombian shore. Given her druthers, she'd have stayed in Barranquilla and waited for Victoria's return. No, she insisted, given her druthers, she'd be working in Philadelphia, patiently waiting for her August break.

But that was neither here nor there. She was on the *Golden Echo*, soon to be well into the Caribbean, and there was no point bemoaning her fate. She had to see the bright side, as Victoria was doing. She'd brought books along, and she'd spotted cushions in the salon that could be used as padding in lieu of a deck chair. And if she worked to keep her presence as inconspicuous as possible, she knew she'd do all right.

"Having second thoughts?"

The low, taunting baritone came from behind her. She didn't have the slightest doubt as to whose voice it was.

"What's to have second thoughts about?" she asked quietly. "This is my vacation. I'm looking forward to it."

"Are you always uptight when you're looking forward to something?"

"I'm not uptight."

He moved forward until he, too, leaned against the wood. "No?"

Shaye was peripherally aware of his largeness and did her best to ignore it. "No."

"Then why are your knuckles white on that rail?"

"Because if the boat lurches, I don't want to be thrown."

"She's called a sloop, and she doesn't lurch."

"Sway, tilt, heel—whatever the term is."

"Not a sailor, I take it?"

"I've sailed."

"Sunfish? Catboat?"

"Actually, I've spent time on twelve-meters, but as a guest, not a student of nautical terminology."

"A twelve-meter is a far cry from the *Golden Echo*."

"Do tell."

"You're not pleased with her?"

"She's fine," Shaye answered diplomatically.

"But not up to your usual standards?"

"I didn't say that."

"You're thinking it. Tell me, if you're used to something faster and sleeker, what are you doing here?"

Shaye bit off the sharp retort that was on the tip of her tongue and instead answered calmly, "As I said, I'm on vacation."

"Why here?"

"Because my aunt invited me to join her."

"And you were thrilled to accept?"

She did turn to him then and immediately wished she hadn't. He towered over her, a good six-four to her own five-six, and there was an air of menace about him. She took a deep breath to regain her poise, then spoke slowly and as evenly as possible.

"No, I was not thrilled to accept. Sailing off in the facsimile of a pirate ship on a wild goose chase for a treasure that probably doesn't exist is not high on my list of ways I'd like to spend my vacation."

Noah's gaze was hard as he studied her face. She was a beauty, but cool, very cool. Her features were set in rigid lines, her hazel eyes cutting. Had he seen any warmth, any softening, he would have eased off. But he was annoyed as hell that she was along, and to have her match his stare with such boldness was just what he needed to goad him on.

"That was what I figured." His eyes narrowed. "Now listen here, and listen good. If you repeat any of those pithy comments within earshot of my uncle, you'll regret it."

The blatant threat took Shaye by surprise. She'd assumed Noah to be rude; she hadn't expected him to be openly hostile. "Excuse me?"

"You heard."

"Heard, but don't believe. What makes you think I'd say anything to your uncle?"

"I know your type."

"How could you possibly—"

"You expected a luxury yacht, not a wreck of a boat. You expected a lovely stateroom, not a small, plain cabin. You expected a captain and a cook, not a professor who's staging Halloween three months early."

Shaye's blood began a slow boil. "You were eavesdropping!"

His eyes remained steady, a chilling gray, and the dark spikes of hair that fell over his brow, seeming to defy the wind, added to the aura of threat that was belied by the complacency of his voice. "I was sitting below while you and your aunt chatted on deck."

"So you listened."

"The temptation was too great. In case you haven't realized it yet, we'll be practically on top of each other for the next two weeks. I wanted to know what I was in for." His gaze dropped to her hands. "I'd ease up if I were you. Those nails of yours will leave marks on the wood."

Shaye's fingernails weren't overly long, though they were neatly filed and wore a coat of clear polish. Instead of arguing, she took yet another deep breath and squared her shoulders. "Thank you for making your feelings clear."

"Just issuing a friendly little warning."

"Friendly?"

"We-e-e-ll, maybe that is stretching it a little. You're too stiff-backed and fussy for my tastes."

Shaye's temper flared. "You have to be one of the most arrogant individuals I've ever had the misfortune to meet. You don't know me at all. You have no idea what I do, what I like or what I want. But I'll tell you one thing, I don't take to little warnings the likes of which you just issued."

"Consider it offered nonetheless."

"And you can consider it rejected." Eyes blazing, she made a slow and deliberate sweep from his thick, dark hair over his faded black T-shirt and worn khaki shorts, down long, hair-roughened legs to his solid bare feet. "I don't need you telling me what to do. I can handle myself and in good taste, which is a sight more than I can say for you." Every bit as deliberately as she'd raked his form, and with as much indifference to his presence as she could muster, she returned her gaze to the shrinking port.

"I'd watch it, if I were you. I'm not in the mood to be crossed."

"Another threat?" she asked, keeping her eyes fixed on the shore. "And what will you do if I choose to ignore it?"

"I'll be your shadow for the next two weeks. I could make things unpleasant, you know."

"I have the distinct feeling you'll do that anyway." Turning, she set off smoothly for the bow.

3

VICTORIA SQUINTED UP at Samson. "How much farther will we be towed?"

"Not much. We're nearly clear of the smaller boats, and the wind is picking up nicely."

Shaye joined them in time to catch his answer. "What happens if it dies once we're free?"

Samson grinned. "Then we'll lie on the deck and bask in the sun until it decides to come back to life."

She had visions of lying in the sun and basking for days, and the visions weren't enticing. Still smarting from her set-to with Noah, she feared that if they were becalmed she'd go stark, raving mad. "Given a reasonable wind, how long will it take to reach Costa Rica?"

"Given a reasonable wind, four days. The *Golden Echo* wasn't built for speed."

"What was she built for?" Shaye asked, her curiosity off-set by a hint of aspersion.

"Effect," came Noah's tight reply as he took up a position beside her.

Her shadow. Was it starting already? Tipping up her head, she challenged him with a stare. "Explain, please."

Noah directed raised brows toward his uncle, who in his own shy way was a storyteller. But Samson shook his head, pivoted on his heel and headed aft, calling over his shoulder, "It's all yours. I have to see to the sails."

Noah would have offered his assistance if it hadn't been for two things. First, Samson would have refused: he took pride in his sailing skill and preferred, whenever possible, to do things himself. Second, Noah wanted to stay by Shaye. He knew that he annoyed her, and he intended to take advantage of that fact. It was some solace, albeit perverse, to have her aboard.

"The *Golden Echo* was modeled after an early eighteenth century Colonial sloop," he began, broadening his gaze to include Victoria in the tale. "She was built in the 1920s by a man named Horgan, a sailor and a patriot, who saw in her lines a classic beauty that was being lost in the sleeker, more modern craft. Horgan wanted to enjoy her, but he also wanted to make a statement."

"He did that," Shaye retorted, then asked on impulse, "Where did he sail her?"

"Up and down the East Coast at first."

"For pleasure?"

Noah's eyes bore into her. "Some people do it that way."

Victoria, who'd been watching the two as she leaned back against the rail, asked gently, "Did he parade her?"

"I'm sure he did," Noah answered, softening faintly with the shift of his gaze, "though I doubt there was as much general interest in a vessel like this then as there is today. From what Samson learned, Horgan made several Atlantic crossings before he finally berthed the *Golden Echo* in Bermuda. When his own family lost interest and he grew too ill to sail her alone, he began renting her out. She was sold as part of his estate in the mid-sixties."

"That leaves twenty years unaccounted for," Shaye prompted.

"I'm getting there." But he took his time, leisurely looking amidship to check on his uncle's progress. By the time he resumed, Shaye was glaring out to sea. "The new owners, a couple by the name of Payne, expanded on the charter business. For a time, they worked summers out of Boston, where the *Golden Echo* was in demand for private parties and small charity functions. Eventually they decided that the season was too limited, so they moved south."

"Why aren't they with us now?" Shaye asked without turning her head.

"Because there isn't room. Besides, they have a number of other boats to manage. The business is headquartered in Jamaica."

"Why are we in Colombia?"

"Because that's where the last charter ended. It's a little like Hertz—"

"Noah!" came Samson's buoyant shout. "Set us free!"

With a steadying hand on the bowsprit, Noah folded himself over the prow, reaching low to release the heavy steel clip that had held the powerboat's line to the *Golden Echo*.

The powerboat instantly surged ahead, then swung into a broad U-turn. Its driver, a Colombian with swarthy skin and a mile-wide white grin, saluted as he passed. A grinning Victoria waved back, moving aft to maintain the contact.

Shaye was unaware of her departure. She hadn't even seen the Colombian. Rather, her eyes were glued to the spot where Noah had released the clip. The large, rusty ring spoke for itself, but what evoked an odd blend of astonishment and amusement was the fact that it protruded from the navel of a scantily clad lady. That the lady was time-worn and peeling served only to accentuate her partial nudity.

"That's the figurehead," Noah informed her, crossing his arms over his chest.

"I know what it is," she answered, instantly losing grasp of whatever amusement she'd felt. "I just hadn't seen her earlier."

"Does her state of undress embarrass you?"

"I've seen breasts before."

Insolent eyes scanned the front of her T-shirt. "I should hope so."

Shaye kept her arms at her sides when they desperately wanted to cover her chest. She was far from the prude that Noah had apparently decided she was, but while she'd learned to control her desires, there was something about the way he was looking at her that set off little sparks inside. She felt nearly as bare-breasted as the lady on the bow and not nearly as wooden—which was something she sought to remedy by turning the tables on Noah.

"Does she excite you?"

"Who?"

Shaye tossed her head toward the bow, then watched as he bent sideways.

"She's not bad," he decided, straightening. "A little stern-faced for my tastes. Like you."

"Your tastes are probably as pathetic as old Horgan's. If he were building a boat like this today and dared to put a thing like that at the bow, he'd have women's groups picketing the pier."

Noah drew himself to his full height and glared down at her. "If there's one thing I can't stand it's a militant feminist."

She glared right back. "And if there's one thing *I* can't stand, it's a presumptuous male. You're just itching for a fight, aren't you?"

"Damn right."

"Why?"

"Why not?"

"The way I see it," she said, taking a deep breath for patience, "either you're annoyed that I've come along or you didn't want to be here in the first place."

His hair was blowing freely now. "Oh, I would have been happy enough sailing off with Samson. He's undemanding. I'd have gotten the R and R I need."

"Then it's me. Why do I annoy you?"

"You're a woman, and you're prissy."

Unable to help herself, Shaye laughed. *"Prissy?"* Then some vague instinct told her that prissy was precisely the way to be with this man. "Prissy." She cleared her throat. "Yes, well, I do believe in exercising a certain decorum."

"I'm sure you give new meaning to the word."

Shaye was about to say that Noah probably didn't know the *first* meaning of the word when the sound of unfurling canvas caught her ear. She looked up in time to see the mainsail fill with wind, then down to see Samson securing the lines.

"Shouldn't you give him a hand?"

"He doesn't need it."

"Then why are you here at all?"

Noah's smile might have held humor but didn't. "To give you a hard time. Why else?" With that, he sauntered off.

Aware that he'd had the last word this time around, Shaye watched him until he disappeared into the companionway. Then she turned back to the bow and closed her eyes. His image remained, a vivid echo in her mind of tousled dark hair, a broad chest, lean hips and endless legs. He was attractive; she had to give him that. But the attraction ended with the physical. He was unremittingly disagreeable.

And exhausting. It had been a long time since she'd sparred with anyone as she was sparring with him. Not that she didn't have occasional differences with people at work, but that was something else, something professional. In her private life she'd grown to love peace. She avoided abrasive people and chose friends who were conventional and comfortable. She dated the least threatening of men, indulging their occasional need to assert themselves over choice of restaurants or theaters because, through it all, she was in control. Not even her parents, with their parochial views, could rile her.

But Noah VanBaar had done just that. She wasn't sure how they'd become enemies so quickly. Was it his fault? Hers? Had she really seemed prissy?

A helpless smile broke across her face. Prissy. Wouldn't André and the guys from the garret—wherever they were today—die laughing if they heard that! Her parents, on the other hand, wouldn't die laughing. They'd choke a little, then breathe sighs of relief, then launch into a discourse on her age and the merits of marriage.

Prissy. It wasn't such a bad thing to be around Noah. If he hated prissiness so much, he'd leave her alone, which was all she really wanted, wasn't it?

Buoyed by her private pep talk, she sought out Victoria, who was chatting with Samson as he hauled up the first of two jibs. Indeed, it was Samson she addressed. "Would you like any help?"

Deftly lashing the line to its cleat, he stood back to watch the sail catch the wind. "Nope. All's under control." He darted them a quick glance. "Have you ladies had breakfast yet?"

"Victoria, has, but I, uh, slept a little later."

"You'll find fresh eggs and bacon in the icebox. Better eat and enjoy before they spoil."

Fresh eggs and bacon sounded just fine to Shaye, even if the word *icebox* was a little antiquated. Somehow, though, coming from Samson it didn't seem strange. Without pausing to reflect on the improvement in her attitude toward him, she asked, "How about you? Can I bring you something?"

"Ah no," he sighed, patting his belt. "I had a full breakfast earlier."

"How about coffee?"

"Now that's a thought. If you make it strong and add cream and two sugars, I could be sorely tempted."

Shaye smiled and turned to her aunt. "Anything for you?"

"Thanks, sweetheart, but I'm fine."

"See you in a bit, then." Still smiling, she entered the companionway, trotted down the steps and turned into the galley. There her smile faded. Noah was sprawled on the built-in settee that formed a shallow U behind the small table. He'd been alerted by the pad of her sneakers and was waiting, fork in hand, chewing thoughtfully.

"Well, well," he drawled as soon as he'd swallowed, "if it isn't the iron maiden."

"I though you'd already eaten."

"Samson has, but I don't make a habit of getting up at dawn like he does."

She was looking at his plate, which still held healthy portions of scrambled eggs and bacon, plus a muffin and a half, and a huge wedge of melon. "Think you have enough?"

"I hope so. I'm going to need all the strength I can get."

"To sit back and watch Samson sail?"

"To fight with you."

Determined not to let him irk her—or to let him interfere with her breakfast—she went to the refrigerator. "It's not really worth the effort, you know."

"I'll be the judge of that."

She shrugged and reached for two eggs and the packet of bacon. After setting them on the stove, she opened one cabinet, then the second in search of a pan.

"In the sink," Noah informed her.

She took in the contents of the sink at a disdainful glance. "And filthy. Thanks."

"You're welcome."

Automatically she reached for the tap, only to find there was none.

"Try the foot pump. You won't get water any other way. Not that you really need it. Why not just wipe out the pan with a paper towel and use it again?"

"That's disgusting."

"Not really. You're having the same thing I had."

"But there's an inch of bacon fat in this pan."

"Drain it."

There was a subtle command in his voice that drew her head around. "I take it we're conserving water."

"You take it right."

She pressed her lips together, then nodded slowly as she considered her options. She could pump up the water in a show of defiance, but if water was indeed in short supply, she'd be biting off her nose to spite her face. Bathing was going to be enough of a challenge; a little water spared now would make her feel less guilty for any she used later.

Very carefully she drained the pan, then swabbed it out with a paper towel and set it on the stove to heat.

"Need any help?" he taunted.

"I can crack an egg."

"Better put on the bacon first. It takes longer."

"I know that."

"Then you'd better start separating the bacon. The pan will be hot and you'll be wasting propane."

"Are you always a tightwad?"

"Only when I'm with a spendthrift."

"You don't know what you're talking about."

"So educate me."

But Shaye wasn't about to do any such thing. It suited her purpose to keep Noah in the dark, just as it suited her purpose to leisurely place one rasher of bacon, then another in the pan. While they cooked, she rummaged through the supplies until she located the coffee, then set a pot on to perk.

"I'm impressed," Noah said around a mouthful of food. "I didn't think you had it in you."

She'd been acutely aware of his eyes at her back, and despite good intentions, her temper was rising. "Shows how much you know," she snapped.

"Then you don't have a cook back in wherever?"

"I don't have a cook."

"How about a husband?"

Without turning, she raised her left hand, fingers rigidly splayed and decidedly bare.

"The absence of a ring doesn't mean anything. Militant feminists often—"

"I am not a militant feminist!" Gripping the handle of the frying pan, she forked the bacon onto its uncooked side. Slowly and silently she counted to ten. With measured movements, she reached for an egg.

It came down hard on the edge of the pan. The yoke broke. The white spilled over the rim.

Repairing the damage as best she could, she more carefully cracked the second egg, then stood, spatula in hand, waiting for both to cook.

"I thought you said you could crack an egg."

She didn't respond to the jibe.

"Got anything planned for an encore?"

She clamped her lips together.

"You could always flip an egg onto the floor."

"Why don't you shut up and eat?"

"I'm done."

Eyes wide, she turned to see that his plate, piled high short moments before, was now empty. "You're incredible."

He grinned broadly. "I know."

Her gaze climbed to his face, lured there by a strange force, one that refused to release her. Even after the slash of white teeth had disappeared, she stared, seeing a boyishness that was totally at odds with the man.

Unable to rationalize the discrepancy, she tore herself away and whirled back to the stove. The tiny whispers deep in her stomach could be put down to hunger, and the faint tremor in her hands as she transferred the eggs and bacon to a dish could be fatigue. But *boyishness*, in *Noah*?

A warning rang in her mind at the same moment she felt a pervasive warmth stretch from the crown of her head to her heels.

"Like I said," Noah murmured in her ear, "I'll need all my strength."

One arm reached to her left and deposited his dish, utensils clattering, in the sink. The other reached to her right and shifted the frying pan to the cold burner. The overall effect was one of imprisonment.

"Do you mind?" she muttered as she held herself stiffly against the stove.

He didn't move. Only his nose shifted, brushing the upper curve of her ear. "You smell good. Don't you sweat like the rest of us?"

Shaye felt a paradoxical dampness in the palms of her hands, at the backs of her knees, in the gentle hollow between her breasts, and was infinitely grateful that he couldn't possibly know. "Would you please move back?" she asked as evenly as she could.

"Have you ever been married?"

"I'd like to eat my eggs before they dry up."

"Got a boyfriend?"

"If you're looking for something to do, you could take a cup of coffee to your uncle."

"You never get those sweet little urges the rest of us get?"

Swinging back her elbow, she made sharp contact with his ribs. In the next instant she was free.

"That was dirty," he accused, rubbing the injured spot as she spun around.

"That was just for starters." Her hands were balled at her sides, and she was shaking. "I don't like to be crowded. Do you think you can get that simple fact through your skull, or is it too much to take in on a full stomach?"

Noah's hand stilled against his lean middle, and he studied her for a long minute. "I think I make you nervous."

"Angry. You make me angry."

"And nervous." He was back to taunting. "You're flushed."

"Anger."

Silkily he lowered his eyes to her left breast. "That, too?"

She refused to believe that he could see the quick quiver of her heart, though she couldn't deny the rapidity of her breathing. Even more adamantly she refused to believe that the tiny ripples of heat surging through her represented anything but fury. "That, too."

His gaze dropped lower, charting her midriff, caressing the bunching of jersey at her waist, arriving at last at her hips. His brow furrowed. He seemed confused yet oddly spellbound. Then, as though suddenly regaining the direction he'd lost, he snapped his eyes back to her face. "Too bad," he said, his lips hardening. "You've got the goods. It's a shame you can't put them to better use."

Shaye opened her mouth to protest his insolence, but he had already turned and was stalking away. "You left your dirty things in the sink!" she yelled.

He didn't answer. His tall frame blended with the shadow of the companionway, then disappeared into the blinding light above.

SOME TIME LATER, bearing cups of coffee for Samson and herself, Shaye returned to the deck. Samson stood at the helm, looking utterly content. He accepted the coffee with a smile, but Shaye didn't stay to talk. He was in his own world. He didn't need company.

Besides, Noah sat nearby. His long legs formed an open circle around a coil of rope and, while his hands were busily occupied, he watched her every move.

So she proceeded on toward the bow, where Victoria leaned against the bulwark gazing out to sea.

"Pretty, isn't it?"

Shaye nodded. The Colombian coast was a dark ridge on the horizon behind. Ahead was open sea. Far in the distance a cargo ship headed for Barranquilla or Cartagena. Less far a trawler chugged along, no doubt from one of the fishing villages along the coast.

Her fancy was caught, though, by a third, smaller craft, a yacht winging through the waters like a slender white dove. Peaceful, Shaye thought. Ahh, what she'd give for a little of that peace.

"Everything okay?" Victoria asked.

"Just fine."

"You look a little piqued."

"I'm tired."

"Not feeling seasick?"

Shaye shot her the wry twist of a grin. "Not quite."

"Have you ever been seasick?"

"Nope."

"Mmm." Victoria shook back her head and tipped it up to the sky. "In spite of everything, you have to admit that this is nice." When Shaye didn't respond, she went on. "It doesn't really matter what boat you're on, the air is the same, the sky, the waves." She slitted one eye toward Shaye. "Still want to go back?"

"It's a little late for that, don't you think?"

"But if you could, would you?"

Shaye dragged in a long, deep breath, then released it in a sigh. "No, Victoria, I wouldn't go back. But that doesn't mean this is going to be easy."

"What happened in the galley?"

Shaye took a deliberately lengthy sip of her coffee. "Nothing."

"Are you sure?"

"I'm sure."

"You sound a little tense."

"Blame that on fatigue, too." Or on anger. Or on frustration. Or, in a nutshell, on Noah VanBaar.

"But it's not even noon."

"It feels like midnight to me. I may go to bed pretty soon."

"But we've just begun to sail!"

"And we'll be sailing for the next four days straight, so there'll be plenty of time for me to take it all in."

"Oh, Shaye . . ."

"If I were in the Berkshires, I'd still be in bed."

"Bo-ring."

"Maybe so, but this is my vacation, isn't it? If I don't catch up on my sleep now, I never will. Weren't you the one who said I could do it on the boat?"

Victoria yielded with grace. "Okay. Sleep. Why don't you drag some cushions up here and do it in the sun?"

Because Noah is on deck and there's no way I could sleep knowing that. "That much sun I don't need."

"Then, the shade. You can sleep in the shade of the sails."

But Shaye was shaking her head. "No, I think I'll try that bed of ours." Her lips twisted. "Give it a test run." She took another swallow of coffee.

Victoria leaned closer. "Running away from him won't help, y'know. You have to let him know that he doesn't scare you."

"He doesn't scare me."

"He can't take his eyes off you."

"Uh-huh."

"It's true. He's been watching you since you came on deck."

"He's worried that I'm going to spoil Samson's trip by saying something ugly."

"He said that?"

"In no uncertain terms."

"What else did he say?" Victoria said, and Shaye realized
she'd fallen into the trap. But it wasn't too late to extricate
herself. She didn't want to discuss Noah with Victoria, who
would, no doubt, play the devil's advocate. Shaye wasn't
ready to believe *anything* good about Noah.

So she offered a cryptic, "Not much."

Victoria had turned around so that her back was to the
bulwark. Quite conveniently, she had a view of the rest of the
boat. "He's very good-looking."

"If you say so," Shaye answered indifferently.

"He appears to be good with his hands."

"I wouldn't know about that."

"Do you have any idea what he does for a living?"

"Nope."

"Aren't you curious?"

"Nope."

"Then you're hopeless," Victoria decided, tossing her
hands in the air and walking away.

"Traitor," Shaye muttered under her breath. "I'm only here
because of you, and are you grateful? Of course not. You
won't be satisfied until I'm falling all over that man, but I can
assure you that won't happen. He and I have nothing in
common. Nothing at all."

THEY DID, as it turned out. Noah was as tired as Shaye. He'd
flown in the day before from New York via Atlanta, where
he'd had a brief business meeting, and rather than going to a
hotel in Barranquilla, he'd come directly to the *Golden Echo*
to help Samson prepare for the trip.

Though he'd never have admitted it aloud, Shaye hadn't been far off the mark when she'd called the boat a wreck. Oh, she was seaworthy; he'd checked for signs of leakage when he'd first come aboard and had found none. The little things were what needed attention—lines to be spliced, water pumps to be primed, hurricane lamps to be cleaned—all of which should by rights have been done before the *Golden Echo* left Jamaica on her previous charter. But that was water over the dam. He didn't mind the work. What he needed now, though, was rest.

"I'm turning in for a while," he told Samson, who was quite happily guarding the helm. "If you need me for anything, give a yell."

The older man kept his eyes on the sea. "Do me a favor and check on Shaye? She went below a little while ago. I hope she's not sick."

Noah knew perfectly well that she'd gone below. He wouldn't have said that she'd looked particularly sick, since she'd seemed pale to him from the start.

"I'd ask Victoria to do it," Samson was saying, "but I hate to disturb her." She was relaxing on the foredeck, taking obvious pleasure in both the sun and the breeze. "Since you're going below anyway..."

"I'll check."

But only because Samson had asked. Left to his own devices, Noah would have let Shaye suffer on her own. His encounter with her in the galley had left him feeling at odds with himself, and though that had been several hours before, he hadn't been able to completely shake the feeling. All he wanted was to strip down and go to sleep without thought of the woman. But Samson had asked...

She wasn't in the galley or the salon, and since she certainly wouldn't be in the captain's quarters, he made for her cabin. The door was shut. He stood for a minute, head bowed, hands on his hips. Then he knocked very lightly on the wood. When there was no answer, he eased open the door.

The sight before him took him totally by surprise. Shaye had pulled back the covers and was lying on her side on the bare sheets, sound asleep. She wore a huge white T-shirt that barely grazed her upper thighs. Her legs were slightly bent, long and slender. But what stunned him most was her hair. It fanned behind her on the pillow, a thick, wavy train of auburn that caught the light off the portholes and glowed.

Fascinated, he took one step closer, then another. She seemed like another woman entirely when she was relaxed. There was gentleness in her loosely resting fingers, softness in her curving body, vulnerability in the slight part of her lips and in the faint sheen of perspiration that made her skin gleam. And in her hair? Spirit. Oh, yes. There it was— promise of the same fire he'd caught from time to time in her eyes.

Unable to resist, he hunkered down by the side of the bed. Her lashes were like dark flames above her cheekbones. Free now of tension, her nose looked small and pert. Her cheeks were the lightest shade of a very natural pink that should have clashed with her hair but didn't. And that hair—he wondered if it were as soft as it looked, or as hot. His fingers curled into his palms, resisting the urge to touch, and he forced his eyes away.

It was a major mistake. The thin T-shirt, while gathered loosely in front, clung to her slender side and the gentle flare of her hip, leaving just enough to the imagination to make him ache. And edging beneath the hem of the shirt was a slash of the softest, sweetest apricot-colored silk. His gaze jumped convulsively to the far side of the bed, where she'd left the clothes she'd discarded. There, lying atop the slacks and T-shirt she'd been wearing earlier, was a lacy bra of the same apricot hue.

With a hard swallow, he flicked his gaze back to her face. Stern, stiff-backed and fussy—was that the image she chose to convey to the world? Her underthings told a different story, one that was enhanced by her sleeping form. It was interesting, he mused, interesting and puzzling.

Image making was his business. He enjoyed it, was good at it. Moreover, knowing precisely what went into the shaping of public images, he prided himself on being able to see through them. He hadn't managed to this time, though, and he wondered why. Was Shaye that good, or had his perceptiveness been muddled?

He suspected it was a little of both, and there was meager comfort in the thought. If Shaye was that good, she was far stronger and more complex than he'd imagined. If his perceptiveness had been muddled, it was either because he was tired . . . or because she did something to his mind.

He feared it was the latter. He'd been ornery because he hadn't wanted her along, but that orneriness had been out of proportion. He didn't normally goad people the way he had her. But Shaye—she brought out the rawest of his instincts.

In every respect. Looking at her now, all soft and enticing, he felt the heat rise in his body as it hadn't done in years. How could he possibly be attracted to as prickly a woman? Was it her softness his body sensed and responded to? Or her hidden fire?

His insides tensed in a different way when her lashes fluttered, then it was too late to escape. Not that he would have, he told himself. He'd never run from a woman, and he wasn't about to now. But he'd be damned if he'd let her know how she affected him. Retrieving his mask of insolence, he met her startled gaze.

Shaye didn't move a muscle. She simply stared at him. "What are you doing here?"

"Checking on you. Samson thought you might be sick."

"I'm not."

"Not *violently* seasick?"

"... No."

His gaze idly scored her body. "Did you lie about anything else?"

Why, she asked herself, did he sound as though he knew something he shouldn't? Victoria would never have betrayed her. And there was no way he could see through her T-shirt, though she almost imagined he had. She'd have given anything to reach for the sheet and cover herself, but she refused to give him the satisfaction of knowing that his wandering eye made her nervous. "No," she finally answered.

"Mmm."

"What is that supposed to mean?"

"That you're a contradiction," he said without hesitation.

He'd obviously been thinking about her—or crouching here, watching her—for some time. The last thought made her doubly nervous, and the explanation he offered didn't help.

"Cactus-prickly when you're awake, sweet woman when you're asleep. It makes me wonder which is the real you."

"You'll never know," she informed him. Her poise was fragile; there was something debilitating about lying on a bed near Noah, wearing not much more than an old T-shirt.

His gray eyes glittered. "It'd be a challenge for me to find out. Mmm, maybe I'll make it my goal. I'll have two full weeks with not much else to do."

Shaye didn't like the sound of that at all. "And what about the treasure you're supposedly seeking?" she demanded.

"Samson's doing the seeking. As far as I'm concerned, there are many different kinds of treasure." He surveyed her body more lazily. "Could be that the one you're hiding is worth more than the one my uncle seeks."

"As though I could hide anything this way," she mumbled.

"Precisely."

"Look, I was sleeping. I happen to be exhausted. Do you think you could find a tiny bit of compassion within that stone-hard soul of yours to leave me be?"

He grinned, wondering what she'd have said if she'd known something else had been close to stone-hard moments before. No doubt she'd have used far more potent words to describe his character. Come to think of it, he wondered how many of those potent words she knew.

"You're really very appealing like this," he said softly. "Much more approachable than before. I like your hair."

"Go away."

"I hadn't realized it was so long. Or so thick. The color comes alive when you let it down like that. Why do you bother to tack it up?"

"To avoid comments like the ones you just made."

"I'd think you'd be flattered."

"I'm not."

"You don't like me," he said with a pout.

"Now you're getting there."

"Is it something I said, something I did?"

She squeezed her eyes shut for a minute, then, unable to bear the feeling of exposure any longer, bolted up and reached for the sheet.

Noah looked as though he'd lost his best friend. "What did you do that for? I wouldn't have touched you."

There was touching and there was touching. He could touch her with his hands, or with his eyes. Or he could touch her with the innocent little expressions he sent her way from time to time. She knew not to trust those little expressions, but, still, they did something to her. Far better that he should be growling and scowling.

"It's your eyes," she accused as she pressed her back to the wall. "I don't like them."

This time his innocence seemed more genuine. "What's wrong with my eyes?"

"They creep."

"They explore," he corrected, "and when they find something they like, they take a closer look." He shrugged. "Can you blame them? Your legs are stunning."

She quickly tucked her legs under her. "Please. Just leave and let me sleep."

Since the path had been cleared for him, he hopped up and sat on the bed.

"Noah . . ." she warned.

"That's the first time you've called me by name. I like it when you say it, though you could soften the tone a little."

"Leave this cabin now!"

He made himself more comfortable, extending an arm, propping his weight on his palm. "You never answered me when I asked about boyfriends. Do you have any back home? Where is home, by the way?"

"Philadelphia," she growled. "There, you've gotten some information. Now you can leave."

"A little more. I want a little more. Is there a boyfriend?"

In a bid for dignity, she drew herself up as straight as she could. Unfortunately he was sitting on the sheet, which ended up stretched taut. And even with the extra inches she felt dwarfed. Why did he have to be so *big*? Why couldn't he be of average height like her lawyer friend, or the stockbroker? For that matter, why couldn't he be malleable, like they were? They'd have left the instant she'd asked *if* they ever made it to her room at all.

"Boyfriends?" he prompted.

"That's none of your business."

"I'll tell you about me if you tell me about you," he cajoled.

"I don't want to know about you."

Bemused, he tipped his dark head to the side. "Wouldn't it be easier if you knew what you faced?"

"I'm not facing anything," she argued, but there was a note of desperation in her voice.

"Two weeks, Shaye. We're going to be together for two long weeks."

"Miss Burke, to you."

For a split second he looked chastised, then spoiled it with a helpless spurt of laughter.

"All right," she grumbled quickly. "Call me Shaye."

"Shaye." He tempered his grin. "Do you have any boyfriends?"

She knew she'd lost a little ground on the Miss Burke bit, which even to her own ears had sounded inane. But she was supposed to be prissy. And as far as boyfriends were concerned, a few white lies wouldn't hurt.

"I don't date."

His eyes widened. "You've got to be kidding."

"No."

"With a body like yours?"

"For your information, there's more to life than sex." She wondered if she was sounding *too* prissy. She didn't want to overdo it.

"Really?"

"I'm too busy to date. I have a very demanding job, and I love it. My life is complete."

He shook his head. "Whew! You're something else." He didn't believe her for a minute, but if she wanted to play games, he could match her. "I have a demanding job myself, but I couldn't make it through life without steady helpings of sex. Women's liberation has its up side, in that sense."

"Then what are you doing on this trip?" she asked through gritted teeth. "How could you drag yourself away from all those warm beds and passionate arms?"

"And legs," he added quickly. "Don't forget legs. I'm a leg man, remember?"

She was getting nowhere, she realized. He looked as though he had no intention of budging, and she didn't think she had the physical strength to make him. "Please," she said, deliberately wilting a little, "I really am tired. I don't want to fight you, and I don't want to be on guard every minute of this trip. If you just leave me alone, I'll stay out of your way."

"Please, Noah."

"Please, Noah."

Her meekness was too much, he decided. When she was meek, there was no fire in her eyes, and he rather liked that fire. "Well, I have learned something new about you."

"What's that?"

His eyes slid over the moistness of her skin. "You sweat."

"Of course I sweat! It's damn hot in here!"

He grinned. So much for meekness. "The question," he ventured in a deep, smooth voice, "is whether you smell as good like this as you did before." He leaned closer.

Shaye put up here hands to hold him off, losing her grip on the sheet in the process. But she'd been right; she was no match for his strength. Her palms were ineffective levers against his chest, and despite her efforts, she felt his face against her neck.

His nose nuzzled her. His lips slid to the underside of her jaw. He opened his mouth and dragged it across her cheek to her ear.

And all the while, Shaye was dying a thousand little deaths because she liked the feel of his mouth on her, she liked it!

"Even . . . better," he whispered hoarsely. His lips nipped at her earlobe, and the hoarse whisper came again. "You smell . . . even better."

Her eyes were shut and her breathing had grown erratic. "Please, stop," she gasped brokenly. "Please, Noah . . ."

He was dizzy with pleasure at the contact, and would have gone on nuzzling her forever had he not caught the trace of fear in her voice. He hadn't heard that before, not fear, and he knew instinctively that there was nothing put on about it. Slowly and with a certain amount of puzzlement, he drew back and searched her eyes. They were wide with fear, yes, but with other things as well. And he knew then, without a doubt, what he was going to do.

He'd leave her now, but he'd be true to his word. He'd spend the next two weeks shadowing her, learning what made her tick. She might in fact be the prissy lady she wanted him to believe she was. Or she might be the woman of passion he suspected she was. In either case, he stirred her. That was what he read in her eyes, and though he wasn't sure why, it was what he wanted.

"Go back to sleep," he said gently as he rose from the bed. He was halfway to the door when he heard her snort.

"Fat chance of that! Can I really believe you won't invade my privacy again? And if I were to fall asleep, I'd have nightmares. Hmph. So much for a lovely vacation. Stuck on a stinking pirate ship with a man who thinks he's God's gift to women—"

Noah closed the door on the last of her tirade and, smiling, sauntered off through the salon.

4

"Ahh, *mes belles amies. Notre dîner nous attend sur le pont. Suivez-moi, s'il vous plaît."*

Shaye, who'd been curled in an easy chair in the salon, darted a disbelieving glance at Victoria before refocusing her eyes on Samson. She'd known he'd been busily working in the galley and that he'd refused their offers of help. But she hadn't expected to be called to the table in flawless French— he was a professor of *Latin*, wasn't he?—much less by a man sporting a bright red, side-knotted silk scarf and a cockily set black beret.

Victoria thought he was precious; eccentric was the word Shaye would choose. But he was harmless, certainly more so than his nephew, she mused, and at the moment she was in need of a little comic relief.

It had been a long afternoon. She hadn't been able to fall back to sleep after Noah had left her cabin, though she'd tried her best. After cursing the sheets, the mattress, the heat and everything else in the room, she'd dressed, reknotted her hair and gone on deck.

Noah hadn't been there—he was sleeping, Samson told her, which had irritated her no end. *He* was sleeping, after he'd ruined her own! She'd seethed for a while, then been gently, gradually, helplessly lulled by the rocking of the boat into a better frame of mind.

And now Samson had called them to dinner. The table, it turned out, was a low, folding one covered by a checkered cloth, and the seats were cushions they carried up from the salon. Noah had lowered the jibs and secured the wheel, dashing Shaye's hope that he'd be too busy sailing to join them. To make matters worse, he crossed his long legs and fluidly lowered himself to the cushion immediately on her left.

The meal consisted of a hearty bouillabaisse, served with a Muscadet wine, crusty French bread and, for dessert, a raspberry tart topped with thick whipped cream. Other than complimenting the chef on his work, Shaye mostly stayed out of the conversation, which involved Samson and Victoria and the other unlikely trips each had taken.

Noah, too, was quiet, but his eyes were like living things reaching out, touching her, daring her to reveal something of herself as Victoria and Samson were doing. Since she had no intention of conforming, she remained quiet and ignored his gaze as best she could.

Samson, bless him, was more than willing to accept help with the cleanup, and Shaye was grateful for the escape. By the time she finished in the galley, she was feeling better.

Armed with a cup of coffee and a book, she settled in the salon. Hurricane lamps provided the light, casting a warm golden glow that she had to admit was atmospheric. In fact, she had to admit that the *Golden Echo* wasn't all that bad. Sails unfurled and full once again, the sloop sliced gently through the waves. A crosswind whispered from porthole to porthole, comfortably ventilating the salon. The mustiness that had bothered Shaye earlier seemed to have disappeared, though perhaps, she reflected, she'd simply grown accustomed to it.

She was well fed. She was comfortable. She was peacefully reading her book. Would a vacation in the Berkshires have been any different? *It's all in the mind, Shaye. Isn't that what Victoria would say? He can only be a threat if you allow it, whereas if you put him from mind, he doesn't exist.*

For a time it worked. She flew through the first hundred pages of her book, finally putting it down when her lids began to droop. Victoria was still on deck. Samson had turned in some time before, intending to sleep until two, when he would relieve Noah at the helm.

Intending to sleep far longer than that, Shaye went to bed herself. When she awoke, though, it wasn't ten in the morning as she'd planned. It was three and very dark, and she was feeling incredibly warm all over.

A fever? Not quite. She'd awakened from a dream of Noah. A nightmare? she asked herself, as she lay flat on her back taking slow, easy breaths to calm her quivering body. Only in hindsight. At the time, it had been an excitingly erotic dream. Even now her skin was damp in response.

It isn't fair, she railed, silently. She could push him from her thoughts when she was awake, but how could she control the demon inside while she slept? And what breed of demon was it that caused her to dream erotic dreams about *any* man? She'd lived wildly and passionately for a time, and the lifestyle left much to be desired. She'd sworn off it. She'd outgrown it. She was perfectly content with what she had now.

Could that demon be telling her something?

Uncomfortable with the direction of her thoughts, she carefully rose from the bed so as not to awaken Victoria, dragged a knee-length sweatshirt over her T-shirt and padded silently to the door.

All was quiet save the slap of the waves against the hull and the sough of the breeze. She passed through the salon and the narrow passageway, sending a disdainful glance toward the door of the captain's cabin, where Noah would no doubt be sleeping by now, and carefully climbed the companionway.

On deck she dropped her head back and let the breeze take her unfettered hair as it would. The sea air felt good against her skin, and the sweatshirt was just loose enough, just warm enough to keep her comfortable. Almost reluctantly she straightened her head and opened her eyes, intending to tell Samson that she would be standing at the bow for a bit.

Only it wasn't Samson at the helm. Though the transom's hanging lamp left his face in shadows, the large frame rakishly planted behind the wheel could belong to no one but Noah.

The image struck her, then, with devastating force. He didn't need a billowing shirt, tight pants, boots and a cross belt. He didn't need anything beyond gently clinging shorts and a windbreaker that was barely zipped. He had the rest— thick hair blowing, broad shoulders set, strong hands on the wheel, bare feet widespread and rooted to the deck. Looking more like a descendant of Fletcher Christian than the nephew of Samson VanBaar, he was a rebel if ever there was one. And his prize? Her peace of mind . . . for starters.

"Welcome," he said with unexpected civility. "You wouldn't by chance care to take the helm for a minute while I go get a cup of coffee?"

She certainly wouldn't have allowed herself to turn tail and run once he'd seen her, but she felt impelled to explain her presence. The last thing she wanted was for him to think she was seeking him out. "I thought this was Samson's shift."

"He's exhausted. I decided to let him sleep a while longer."

"You seem tired yourself," she heard herself say. He certainly didn't *sound* like a rebel just then.

He shrugged. "I'll sleep later."

Nodding, she looked away. Something had happened. It was as though the intimacy they'd shared in her dream had softened her. Or was it his fatigue, which softened *him*? Or the gently gusting night air? Or the hypnotic motion of the sloop? Or the fact that starlit nights in the Caribbean were made, in the broadest sense, for love, not war?

Whatever, she turned and started back down the companionway.

"Don't go," he said quickly.

"I'll bring up some coffee."

It was an easy task to reheat what was in the pot. When she returned a few minutes later carrying two mugs, Noah accepted his with a quiet, "Thank you."

Nodding, Shaye stepped back to lean against the transom. For a time, neither spoke. Noah's eyes were ahead, Shaye's were directed northward.

Philadelphia seemed very far away, and it occurred to her that she didn't miss it. Nor, she realized, did she regret the fact that she wasn't heading for the Berkshires. Come light of day, she might miss both, but right now, she felt peaceful. Sated. As though . . . as though her dream had filled some need that she'd repressed. She felt as though she'd just made love with Noah, as though they were now enjoying the companionable afterglow.

"Couldn't sleep?" he asked quietly.

"I, uh, it must have been the rest I had earlier."

"That'll do it sometimes."

They relapsed into silence. Shaye sipped her coffee. Noah did the same, then set the mug down and consulted his compass.

"I was wondering about that," she ventured. "I didn't see any navigational equipment when Samson showed us around."

"I'm not sure what was available when Horgan built the sloop in the twenties, but I assume he felt—and the Paynes must have agreed—that fancy dials would have been sacrilegious." He made a slight adjustment to the wheel, then beckoned to her. "Hold it for a second?"

Setting the mug by her feet, she grasped the wooden wheel with both hands while he moved forward to adjust the sails.

When he returned, though, it was to take the place she'd left at the transom, slightly behind her, slightly to the right.

"So you use a compass?"

"And a sextant. My uncle's the expert with that."

"Is there a specific point we're aiming at?"

Noah took a healthy swallow of his coffee. "He has coordinates, if that's what you mean."

"For the treasure?"

"Uh-huh."

She was looking ahead, holding the wheel steady, assuming that Noah would correct her if she did something wrong. "He hasn't said much about that."

"He's a great one for prioritizing. First, the sail. Then the treasure."

She felt a nudge at her elbow and turned to find him holding out her mug. She took it and lifted it, but rather than drinking, she brushed her lips back and forth against the rim. "It's strange . . ."

"What?"

"That Samson should be a Latin professor and yet have such a proclivity for adventure. Not that I'm being critical. I just find it . . . curious."

"Not really," Noah said. He paused for a minute, deciding how best to explain. "It's a matter of having balance in one's life. Samson has his teaching, which is stable, and his adventures, which are a little more risqué. But there's a link between the two. For example, he sees the same beauty in Latin that he sees in this sloop. They're both ancient—forefathers of other languages, other boats. They both have an innate beauty, a romanticism. Samson is a romantic."

"I hadn't noticed," Shaye teased.

Belatedly, Noah chuckled. "Mmm. He must seem a little bizarre to you."

"No. He's really very sweet."

"He stages Halloween year-round."

She wondered if she'd ever live down that particular comment, but since Noah didn't seem to be angry anymore, there was no point in defending herself. "So I gather," she said with a little grin.

Noah was content with that. "Samson has always believed in doing what he loves. He loves teaching." Reaching out, he rescued a blowing strand of her hair from her mouth and tucked it behind her ear. "He takes delight in making the language come alive for his students. And he does it. I've sat in on some of his classes. In his own quiet way, he is hilarious."

Shaye could believe it. "His stories are something else."

"You were listening?"

She shot him a quick glance. "Tonight? Of course I was."

"I wasn't sure. You were very quiet."

She wasn't about to say that listening hard to Samson had kept her mind off *him*. "Why interrupt something good when you have nothing better to add? It's really a shame that Samson doesn't write about his adventures. They'd make wonderful reading."

"They do."

"Magazine articles?" she asked with some excitement, immediately conjuring up images of a beautiful *National Geographic* spread.

"Books."

"No kidding!"

"How do you think he pays for these little adventures?"

"I really hadn't thought about it." She frowned. "He didn't say anything tonight about writing."

"He's an understated man. He downplays it."

"Can he do that? Isn't there a certain amount of notoriety that comes with being a published author?"

Noah leaned forward and lowered his voice to a conspiratorial level. "Not if you publish under another name." He leaned back again.

"Ahh. So that's how he does it."

"Mmm." He took another drink. "But don't tell him I told you."

She grinned. "Can I ask him where he learned to cook?"

"Cooking he'll discuss any day. It's one of his passions."

Passions. The word stuck in Shaye's mind, turning slowly, a many-faceted diamond with sides of brilliance, darkness, joy and grief.

She shook her hair back, freeing it for the caress of the wind. "You and he seem to be very close. Do you live in Hanover?"

It was a minute before Noah heard the question. He was fascinated by the little movement she'd made. It had been totally unaffected but beguiling. Bare-legged as she was, and with that gorgeous mane of hair—soft, oh yes, soft—blowing behind her, she didn't look anything like the prissy little lady he'd accused her of being.

He closed his eyes for a second and shook off both images, leaving in their place the same gentle ambiance that had existed before. Did he live near Samson in Hanover? "No. But we see each other regularly. There's just him and me. All the others are gone. We have a mutual-admiration society, so it works out well."

"All the others—you mean, your parents?"

"And Samson's wife. Samson and Gena never had children of their own, and since Samson and my father had no other siblings, I was pretty much shared between them."

She smiled. "That must have been fun."

"It was."

She thought about her own childhood, the time she'd spent with her parents. Fun wasn't a word she'd ever used to describe those days. "Was your father as much of a character as Samson?"

"No. He was more serious. Dividing my time between the two men gave a balance to my life, too."

It was the second time he'd spoken of balance, and she wondered if he'd done it deliberately. Her life was far from balanced. Work was her vocation, her avocation, the sole outlet for her energies. Victoria argued that there was more to life, and Shaye smiled and nodded and gave examples of the men she dated and the friends she saw. But apart from her friendship with her sister, the others were largely token friendships. And she knew why. To maintain a steady keel in her life, she chose to be with people who wouldn't rock the boat. Unfortunately, those people were uninspiring. They left her feeling alone and frustrated. Her only antidote was work.

But Noah couldn't possibly know all that, could he?

Feeling strangely empty, she took a large gulp of her coffee, then set the mug down and grasped the wheel more firmly. But neither the solidity of the hard wood nor the warm brew settling in her stomach could counter the chill she was feeling. Unconsciously, she rubbed one bare foot over the other.

In the next instant a third foot covered hers, a larger, warmer one. And then a human shield slipped behind her, protecting her back, her hips, her legs from elements that came from far beyond the Caribbean.

Noah had surrounded her this way in the galley, but the sense of imprisonment was far different now. It was gentle, protective and welcome.

She closed her eyes when she felt his face in her hair, and whispered, "Why are you being so nice?"

His voice was muffled. "Maybe because I'm too tired to fight."

"Then the secret is keeping you tired?"

"The secret," he said as his lips touched her ear, "is keeping your hair down and your legs bare and your mouth sweet. I think something happens when you screw back your hair and cinch yourself into your clothes. Everything tightens up. Your features stiffen and your tongue goes tart."

"It does not!" she cried, but without conviction. She couldn't believe how wonderful she felt, and she wasn't about to deny it any more than she could think to end it. When his face slid to her neck, she relaxed her head against his shoulder.

"I won't argue," he murmured thickly. "Not now."

"You're too tired."

"Too content."

He was pressing open-mouthed kisses to the side of her neck, inching his way lower to the spot where her sweatshirt began. She felt a trembling start at her toes and spread upward, and she grasped the wheel tighter, though she wasn't about to move.

He shifted behind her, spreading his legs to cradle her at the same time his hands fell to her thighs and began to work their way upward.

"Noah . . ." she whispered.

"So soft..." His fingers were splayed, thumbs dragging up along the crease where her thighs met her hips, tracing her pelvic bones, etching a path over her waist and ribs. Then his fingers came together to cup her breasts, and she went wild inside. She arched into his hands, while her head came around, mouth open, tongue trapped against his jaw.

She was melting. Every bone in her body, every muscle, every inch of flesh seemed to lose definition and gather into a single yearning mass. Had she missed this so, this wonderful sense of anticipatory fulfillment? Had she ever experienced it before?

He was roughly caressing her breasts, but it wasn't enough, and her mouth, with hungry nips at his chin, told him so. Then her mouth was being covered, eaten, devoured, and she was taking from him, taste for taste, bite for bite.

Totally oblivious to her role at the helm she wound her arms backward, around Noah. Her hands slid up and down the backs of his thighs, finally clasping his buttocks, urging his masculine heat closer to the spot that suddenly and vividly ached.

"Oh God," he gasped, dragging his mouth from hers. He wrapped quivering arms tightly around her waist and breathed raggedly as his pelvis moved against her. "Ahh . . ."

More hungry than ever, Shaye tried to turn. She wanted to wrap her arms around his neck, to feed again from his mouth, to drape her leg over his and feel his strength where she craved it so. But he wouldn't have it. He squeezed her hard to hold her still, and the movement was enough to restore the first fragments of reason. When he felt that she'd regained a modicum of control, he eased up his hold, but he didn't release her.

With several more gusts of wind, their breathing, their pulse rates, began to slow.

Shaye was stunned. It wasn't so much what had happened but the force with which it had happened that shocked her most. She didn't know what to say.

Noah did, speaking gently and low. "Has it been a long time?"

She'd returned a hand to the wheel, though her fingers were boneless. "Yes," she whispered.

"It took you by surprise?"

Another whispered, "Yes."

"Will you be sorry in the morning?"

"Probably."

He released her then, but without anger. When he reached for the wheel, she stepped aside. "Go below ... please?" he asked gruffly.

She knew what he was doing, and she was grateful. He was alerting her to the fact that if she stayed she might have even more to be sorry for in the morning. She'd felt his arousal; she'd actively fed it. She had to accept her share of responsibility for what had happened, just as she had to respect the pleading note in his voice. He was human. He wanted her. And he was asking her not to want him back ... at least, not tonight.

Without saying a word, she climbed down the companionway. At the bottom, she gasped, a helpless little cry.

"I frightened you," Samson said. "I'm sorry. You seemed very deep in thought."

She was, but her heart was pounding at thoughts that had taken a sudden turn. *What if Samson had awakened earlier and come up on deck during ... during ...*

"I should have been up a while ago," he was saying. "Noah must be exhausted. I'm glad he wasn't alone all that time."

Shaye wasn't sure whether to be glad or not. As she made her silent way to the cabin, then stole back into bed, she wasn't sure of much—other than that she'd be furious with herself later.

SHE WAS FURIOUS. She didn't sleep well, but kept waking up to recall what had happened, to toss and turn for a while, then bury her face in the pillow and plead for the escape of sleep. Mercifully, Victoria was gone from the cabin by seven, which meant that Shaye could do her agonizing in peace.

She slept. She awoke. She slept again, then awoke again. The cycle repeated itself until nearly noon, when she gave up one battle to face the next.

Noah was in the galley. All she wanted was a cup of coffee, but even that wasn't going to be easy.

"Sleep well?" he asked in a tone that gave nothing away.

"Not particularly."

"Bad dreams?"

"It was what was *between* the dreams that was bad," she muttered, pouring coffee into a cup with hands that shook.

"Are you always this cheerful in the morning?"

"Always."

"If you'd woken up in bed with me, it might have been different."

Bracing herself against the stove, she squeezed her eyes shut and made it to the count of eight before his next sally came.

"I'll bet you're dynamite in bed."

She went on counting.

"You were dynamite on the deck."

She cringed. "Don't remind me."

"Are you schizophrenic?"

At that, she turned and stared. "Excuse me?"

"Do you have two distinct personalities?"

"Of course not!"

"Then why are you so crabby this morning when you were so sweet last night?" He gave her a thorough once-over, then decided, "It *has* to be the clothes. You're wearing shorts, but they must be binding somewhere." Her T-shirt was big enough for *him* to swim in, so it couldn't be that. "And your hair. Safely secured once again. Does it make you *feel* secure when it's pinned back like that?"

She grabbed her coffee and made for the salon.

He was right behind her. "Careful. You're spilling."

She whirled on him, only to gasp when several drops of coffee hit his shirt.

He jumped back. "Damn it, that's hot!"

She hadn't intended to splatter him. Without thinking, she reached out to repair the damage.

He pushed her hand away. "It's all right."

"Are you burned?" she asked weakly.

"I'll live."

"The coffee will stain if you don't rinse it out."

"This shirt has seen a lot worse."

Eying the T-shirt, Shaye had to agree. She guessed that it had been navy once upon a time, but no longer. It was ragged at the hem and armholes, and it dipped tiredly at the neck, but damn if it didn't make him look roguish!

Sighing unsteadily, she moved more carefully into the salon and sank into a chair. Her head fell back and she closed her eyes. She felt Noah take the seat opposite her.

"Why are you doing this to me?" she whispered.

He didn't have to think about it, when he'd done nothing else for the past few hours. "You intrigue me."

It wasn't the answer she wanted. "I didn't think you were intrigued by cactus prickly women."

"Ahh, but are you really cactus prickly? That's the question."

"I'm prissy."

"Really?"

"You said it yourself."

"Maybe I was wrong."

"You weren't."

"Could've fooled me last night."

Eyes still closed, she scrunched up her face. "Do you think we could forget about last night?"

"Jeeez, I hope not. Last night was really something."

She moaned his name in protest, but he turned even that to his advantage.

"You did that last night and I liked it. You wanted me. Was that so terrible?"

Her eyes shot open and she met his gaze head-on. "I do not want you."

"You did then."

"I was too tired to know what I was doing."

He was sitting forward, fingers loosely linked between spread knees. "That's just the point. Your defenses were down. Maybe that's the real you."

"The real me," she stated as unequivocally as she could, "is what you see here and now." She had to make him believe it. She had to make *herself* believe it. "I live a very sane, very structured, very controlled existence."

"What fun's that?"

"It's what I choose. You may say its boring, but it's what *I* choose!"

"Is that why you burst into flames in my arms?"

She was getting nowhere. She'd known from the moment she'd left the deck so early this morning that she was in trouble, and Noah wasn't helping. But then, she hadn't really expected he would. So she closed her eyes again and tuned him out.

"You were hungry."

She said nothing.

He upped the pressure. "Sex starved."

Still silence.

He pursed his lips. "You can't seduce Samson because he has his eye on your aunt, so that leaves only me."

"I wouldn't know how to seduce a man if I tried," she mumbled. It fit in with the image of prissiness, but it was also the truth. She'd never had to seduce a man. Sex had been free and easy in the circles she'd run in. Perhaps that was why it had held so little meaning for her. Last night—this morning—had been different. She was still trying to understand how.

"I told you. All you have to do is bare those legs, shake out that hair and say something sweet." He shifted and grimaced. "Lord, you're only one-third of the way there, and I'm getting hard."

Her eyes flew open. "You're crude."

He considered that. "Crude connotes a raw condition. Mmm, that's pretty much the same thing as being hard."

She bolted from the chair and stormed toward her cabin.

"You can't hide there all day, y'know!" he called after her.

"I have no intention of hiding here," she yelled back. "I'm getting a book—" she snatched it from her suitcase, which, standing on end, served as a makeshift nightstand "—and I'm going on deck." She slammed past Noah back through the salon, then momentarily reversed direction to grab a cushion from the sofa.

"You can't escape me there," he warned.

"No," she snapped as she marched down the alley toward the companionway, "but with other people around, you might watch your tongue."

He was on her heels. "I'd rather watch yours. I liked what it did to me last night."

"This morning." She stomped up the steps. "It was this morning, and I can guarantee it won't happen again."

"Don't do that," he pleaded, once again the little boy with the man's mind and body. "You really turned me on—"

"Shh!" She whipped her head around to give him a final glare, then with poise emerged topside, smiled and said, "Good morning, Samson."

NOAH STOOD AT THE WHEEL, his legs braced apart, his fingers curled tightly around the handles. Steering the *Golden Echo* didn't take much effort, but it gave him a semblance of control. He needed that. He wasn't sure why, but he did.

Shifting his gaze from the ocean, he homed in on Shaye. She was propped on a cushion against the bulwark in the shade of the sails, reading. Her knees were bent, her eyes never left the page. Not a single, solitary strand of hair escaped its bonds to blow free in the breeze.

Prickly. God, was she prickly! She was the image of primness, but he knew there was another side. *He* knew it. She refused to admit it. And the more he goaded her, the more prickly she became.

He was no stranger to women. Granted, he wasn't quite the roué he'd told Shaye he was, but his work brought him into contact with women all the time. He'd known charming ones, spunky ones, aggressive and ambitious ones. Shaye was as beautiful as any of them—or, he amended, she was when she let go. She'd done it last night, but it had been dark then. He wanted to see her do it now. If she freed her hair from its knot, relaxed her body, tossed back her head and smiled, he knew he'd take her image to his grave.

But she wouldn't do that. She wouldn't give him the satisfaction. He recalled the times when they'd bickered, when she'd bitten back retorts, taken deep breaths, done everything in her power to ignore his taunts. Sometimes she'd lost control and had lashed back in turn, but even then she'd been quick to regain herself.

What had she said—that she lived a structured and controlled existence? Beyond that he didn't know much, other than that she was from Philadelphia and that she had neither a husband nor a cook. He did know that she was aware of him physically. She couldn't deny what had happened right here, on this very spot, less than twelve hours before.

Nor could he deny it. He knew he was asking for trouble tangling with a woman who clearly had a hang-up with sex. But sex wasn't all he wanted. She intrigued him; he hadn't lied about that. He felt a desperate need to understand her, and that meant getting to know her. And *that* meant breaking through the invisible wall she'd built.

As he saw it, there were two ways to go about it. The first, the more civil way, was to simply approach her and strike up conversation. Of course, it would take a while to build her trust, and if she resisted him he might run out of time.

The second, the more underhanded way, was to keep coming at her as he'd been doing. She wouldn't like it, but he might well be able to wear her down. Since she was vulnerable to him on a physical level, he could prey on that—even if it meant prying out one little bit of personal information at a time.

He had to get those bits of information. Without them, he couldn't form a composite of her, and without that, he wouldn't be able to figure out why in the hell he was interested in the first place!

"HOW'S IT GOING, ladies?"

Shaye looked up from her book to see Noah approach. So he'd finally turned the sailing over to Samson. She had to admit, albeit begrudgingly, that he was doing his share.

"I should ask you the same question," Victoria said, smiling up in welcome. "Are we making good progress?"

Noah looked out over the bow toward the western horizon. "Not bad. If the trade winds keep smiling and we continue to make five knots an hour, we'll reach Costa Rica right on schedule."

Shaye was relieved to hear that.

Victoria wasn't so sure. "I'm enjoying the sail," she said, stretching lazily. "I could take this for another month."

Noah chuckled, then turned to Shaye. "How about you? Think you could take it for another month?"

Had it not been for that knowing little glint in his eye, Shaye might have smiled and nodded. Instead, she boldly returned his gaze and said, "Not on your life. I have to be back at work."

He hunkered down before her, balancing on the balls of his feet. "But if you were to stretch your imagination a little and pretend that work wasn't there, could you sail on and on?"

She crinkled her nose. "Nah. I'm a landlubber at heart. Give me a little cottage in the Berkshires and I'd be in heaven."

"Not heaven, sweetheart," Victoria scoffed. "You'd be in solitary confinement."

"Is that what she usually does for her vacations?" Noah asked.

"What I usually do—"

"That's what she would have been doing this year if I hadn't suggested she come with me."

"Suggested! That's—"

"I can understand what she sees in it," Noah interrupted blithely, ignoring both Shaye and her attempts to speak. "I have my own place in southern Vermont. I don't usually make it there for more than a few days at a stretch, but those few days are wonderful. There's nothing like time spent alone in a peaceful setting to replenish one's energies."

Victoria disagreed. "No, no. Time spent with someone special—that's different. But alone?"

"You spent time alone," Shaye argued hurriedly before someone cut her off.

"Naturally. I can't be with people all the time. But to choose to go off alone—just for the sake of being alone—for days at a time isn't healthy. It says something about your life, if you need that kind of escape."

"We all need escapes from habit," Noah reasoned, "don't we, Shaye?"

He'd tagged on the last in an intimate tone, leaving no doubt in Shaye's mind that he was referring to what had happened between them beneath the stars.

"Victoria is right. Certain kinds of escape are unhealthy."

"But, hot damn, they're fun," he countered in that same low tone.

Victoria looked from one to the other. "Am I missing something?"

"You missed it but good," Noah said with a grin. His eyes were fixed on Shaye. "We had quite a time of it last night—"

"Noah—"

"You did? Shaye, you didn't *tell* me."

Shaye couldn't believe what was happening. "What Noah means is that we had a little disagreement—"

"Only after the fact. It wasn't a disagreement at the time."

Turning to Victoria, Shaye affected a confident drawl. "He gets confused. Poor thing, he's so used to being ornery that it doesn't faze him."

"What happened last night?"

"Nothing hap—"

"You stole out while I was asleep, clever girl." She turned to Noah. "I hope she didn't shock you."

"As a matter of fact—"

"Please!" Shaye cried. "Stop it, both of you!" In her torment she shifted her legs, the better to brace herself.

Noah's gaze shifted too.

She snapped her knees together.

With an almost imperceptible sigh of regret, he dipped his head to the side. "Your niece has beautiful hair, Victoria. It's thick and rich like yours, but the color—where did she get the color?"

"Her father is a flaming redhead. When Shaye was a child—"

"That's enough, Victoria."

Victoria ignored her. "When she was a child, hers was nearly as red as his."

"Does she get her temper from him, too?"

"What do *you* think?"

"Victoria, if you—"

"I think she does," Noah decided with a grin that turned wry. "I'm not sure if I should thank him or curse him."

"You should leave him out of this," Shaye cried.

"Now, now, Shaye," Victoria soothed, "no need to get upset."

Noah added, "I want to know about him. You're much too closemouthed, Shaye. In all the talking we've done, you've barely said a word about yourself."

"Shame on you, Shaye," Victoria chided. "You act as though you have something to hide."

It was a challenge, well intended but a challenge nonetheless. If Shaye denied that she had anything to hide, she'd have to answer Noah's questions. If she came right out and said that she *did* have something to hide, he'd be all the more curious. For a long minute she glared at her aunt, then at Noah, but she still didn't know what to do.

At last Noah took pity. At least, he mused mischievously, he was willing to defer the discussion of her parents until later. But he wasn't about to miss out on another golden opportunity.

In a single fluid movement, he was sitting by her side against the bulwark. "What say we go for a swim later?"

She didn't answer at first. Her right side was tingling—her arm, her hip, everywhere his body touched. She cleared her throat and looked straight ahead. "Be my guest."

"I said 'we.'"

"Thanks, but I don't care to be left in the water while the boat sails on ahead." Implied was that she wouldn't mind if *he* was left behind.

He ruled out that possibility. "We'll lower the sails and drift. The *Golden Echo* won't go anywhere, and we can play."

With one finger he blotted the dampness from her upper lip. "It'll be fun."

She was afraid to move. "I'll watch."

"But the water will feel great." He pried his back from the bulwark. "My shirt's sticking. You'd think the breeze would help."

"You're too hot for your own good."

"I don't know about that," he said in a sultry tone, "but I am hot." Without another word, he leaned forward and peeled off his shirt.

Shaye nearly died. She'd never seen a back as strong and as well formed, and when he relaxed against the bulwark again, the sight of his broad, leanly muscled chest was nearly more than she could bear. She swallowed down a moan.

"Did you say something?" he queried innocently.

"No, no."

"Your voice sounds strange. Higher than usual."

"It's the altitude. We must be climbing."

"We're at sea level."

"Oh. Mmm. That's right."

Without warning he stole her hand, linked their fingers together and placed them on his bare thigh. Then he looked at Victoria. "Maybe you'd like to join us for that swim."

Victoria grinned. "I'd like that."

"'Course, if you come, I'll have to behave."

Shaye grunted. "Like you're doing now?" She tried to pull her hand away but only succeeded in getting a better feel of his warm, hair-roughened thigh.

He feigned hurt. "I'm behaving."

"You're half-naked."

"I'm also half-dressed. Would you rather I'd left on my shirt and taken off my shorts?"

Victoria laughed. He was outrageous! And still he went on, this time turning injured eyes her way.

"I beg your pardon, Victoria. Are you suggesting that I have something to be ashamed of?"

Unable to help herself, she was laughing again. "Of course not. I—"

"This is no laughing matter! You wound my pride!"

"No, no, Noah," she managed to gasp. "I didn't intend—"

"But the damage is done," he said with such an aggrieved expression that she burst into another peal of laughter, which only made him square his chin more. "I can guarantee you that I'm fully equipped."

"I'm sure—"

"You don't believe me," he said in a flurry. He looked at Shaye. "You don't believe me either." He dropped his hand. "Well, I'll show you both!" He had the drawstring of his shorts undone and his thumbs tucked under the waistband before Shaye pressed a frantic hand to his belly.

"Don't," she whispered. "Please?"

Never in his life had Noah seen as beseeching a look. Her hand was burning a hole in him, but she seemed not to notice. She was near tears.

In that moment he lost his taste for the game. "I was only teasing," he said gently.

She looked at him for a minute longer, her eyes searching his face, moving from one feature to another. Her lower lip trembled.

Then she was up like a shot, running aft along the deck and disappearing down the companionway.

He started after her, but Victoria caught his hand. "Let her be for a while. She has to work some things out for herself."

"I don't want to hurt her."

"I know that. I trust you. Your uncle is a talker once he gets going. He's proud of you, and with good reason."

Noah frowned. "When did he do all this talking?" His eyes widened. "While we were on deck last night?"

"While *we* were on deck this *morning*," she answered, grinning mischievously. "You and Shaye sleep late. Samson and I wake up early."

"Ahh," Noah said, but his frown returned. "I'm trying to understand Shaye, but it's tough. She doesn't like to talk about herself."

"She's trained herself to be that way."

He wanted to ask why, just as he wanted to ask Victoria about all those other things Shaye wouldn't talk about. But it wasn't Victoria's place to talk. What was happening here was between Shaye and him. Sweet as she was, Victoria wasn't part of it, and he refused to put her in the position of betraying her niece.

"She'll tell you in time," Victoria said.

"How can you be sure?"

"I know, that's all. Be patient."

Thrusting a hand through his hair, he realized that he had no other choice. With a sigh, he scooped up his shirt and started off.

"Noah?"

He turned.

She dropped a deliberate glance to his shorts, which, without benefit of the drawstring, had fallen precariously low on his hips.

"Oh." He tied the string almost absently, then continued on.

So comfortable with his body, Victoria mused. *So comfortable with his sexuality. If only he could teach Shaye to be that way. . . .*

5

NOAH WAS RIGHT, Shaye knew. She couldn't hide in her cabin forever. It had been childish of her to run off that way, but at the time she'd been unable to cope with the feelings rushing through her. Noah had been so close, so bare, so provocative, and she was so drawn to him on a physical level that it frightened her to tears.

Brash and irreverent, impulsive and uninhibited, he was on the surface everything she tried to avoid. What was beneath the surface, though, was an enigma. She didn't know much about him—what he did for a living, whether he was attached in any manner to a woman, where his deepest needs and innermost values lay. She wanted to label him as all bad, but she couldn't. He was incredibly devoted to Samson and unfailingly kind to Victoria, and that had to account for something.

So. Here she sat—eyes moist, palms clammy, feeling perfectly juvenile. A reluctant smile played along her lips. Was this the adolescence she'd never had? She'd matured with such lightning speed that she'd never had time to feel growing pains—as good a term as any to describe what she was feeling now. She was being forced to reevaluate her wants and needs. And it was painful.

But nothing was accomplished sitting here. She wasn't an adolescent with the luxury of wallowing for hours in self-pity. Her wisest move, it seemed, would be to pull herself together, rejoin the others and try to regain a little of her self-esteem. She would sort things out in time.

Changing into a bathing suit, she unknotted her hair, brushed it out, then caught it up into a ponytail at her crown. After splashing her face with water, she belted on a short terry-cloth robe and left the cabin.

Noah was waiting in the salon, sitting in one of the chairs. She stopped on the threshold and eyed him uncertainly. He didn't comment on her outfit, or on her bare legs, or on her hair. In fact, he seemed almost as uncertain as she, which was just the slightest bit bolstering.

"You said something about going swimming," she reminded him softly.

He sat still for another minute, his face an amalgam of confusion, hesitation and hope. "You want to?" he cautiously asked.

She nodded.

With the blink of an eye, his grin returned, "You're on." He stood and headed for his cabin. "Stay put. I'll just change into trunks and we'll be ready."

"But the sails—"

"Tell Samson to take them in. He'll be game; he loves to swim. And tell Victoria to change, too. She wanted to come."

The door of the aft cabin closed. Shaye watched it for a minute, then walked quietly past and started up the companionway. She wondered about the way he'd been sitting in the salon, about the uncertainty she'd read on his face. That was a side of him she'd never seen, one she hadn't thought existed. It was a far cry from the smugness—or arrogance or annoyance—he usually granted her, and even his returning confidence was somehow different and more manageable. If only she knew what was going on in his head . . .

Noah hung a rope ladder off the port quarter and let Shaye climb down first. She went about halfway before jumping. In the very first instant submerged, she realized by contrast how hot and grubby she'd felt before. Her sense of exhilaration was nearly as great as her sense of refreshment.

Ducking under a second time, she came up with her head back and a smile on her face. She opened her eyes in time to see Noah balance on the transom for an instant before soaring up, out, then down, slicing neatly into the waves. Feeling incredibly light, she treaded water until he appeared by her side.

"Not bad," she said, complimenting his dive.

"Not bad, yourself," he said, complimenting her smile. Then he took off, stroking strongly around the *Golden Echo*'s stern, then along her starboard side. Shaye followed a bit more slowly, but he was waiting for her at the bow before starting down the port side.

Completing the lap, he turned to her with a grin. "You're a good swimmer. It must be that suit you're wearing. It covers up enough of your body. Is it covering up a flotation device, too?"

She rolled her eyes. "Fifteen minutes."

"Fifteen minutes, what?"

"That's how long you made it without a snippy comment. But now you've blown it, and by insulting my suit, no less! There is nothing wrong with this suit." It was, in fact, a designer maillot that she'd paid dearly for.

He sank beneath the surface for a minute, tossing his hair back with a flourish when he came up. "I was hoping to see more of your body. I was hoping for a bikini."

"Sorry," she said, then turned and swam off.

He'd caught up to her in a minute. "You are not sorry. You take perverse pleasure in teasing me."

"Look who's talking!"

"But you're so teasable," he argued, eyes twinkling. "You rise to my taunts."

"No more," she decided and propelled herself backward.

He negated the distance with a single stroke. "Wanna test that out?"

"Sure." She turned sideways and tipped up her nose in an attempt to look imperturbable. It was a little absurd given the steady movement of her arms and legs, but she did her best.

Noah went underwater.

She waited, eventually darting a sidelong glance to where he'd gone down, then waited again, certain that any minute she'd feel a tug at her leg. When she felt so such thing, she glanced to the other side.

No Noah. No bubbles. Nothing but gentle waves.

Vaguely concerned, she made a complete turn. When she saw no sign of him, she submerged for an underwater look. Nothing!

"Noah?" she called, reaching the surface again. "Noah!"

Samson's head appeared over the side of the boat. "Problem, Shaye?"

Her heart was thudding. "It's Noah! He went under and I can't find him!"

Samson cocked his head toward the opposite side of the boat. "Try over here," he said and disappeared.

Performing a convulsive breast stroke, Shaye sped to the port side, to find Noah riding the waves on his back, eyes closed, basking in the sun.

"You bastard!" she screamed, furiously batting water his way. "You terrified me!"

His serenity ruined by her splashing, he advanced on her, turning his face one way then the other against her wet attack. Then he cinched an arm around her waist and drew her against him, effectively stopping the barrage.

"Y'see?" he gloated. "It worked."

"That was a totally stupid thing to do!" she cried, tightly clutching his shoulders. "And irresponsible! What if something really had happened to you? I'm not a trained lifesaver. I couldn't have helped! And think of *me*. I could have gone under looking for you and stayed there too long. You would never have known I was drowning, because you were out of sight, on the far side of the boat, playing your silly little game."

"Samson was keeping an eye on you."

"That's not the point!" She narrowed her eyes. "Next time I won't even bother to look. You know what happened to the little boy who cried wolf?"

"But I'm not a little boy."

She snorted.

His arm tightened. "Wrap your legs around my waist."

"Are you kidding?"

"I'll keep us afloat."

"I don't trust you."

"You don't trust yourself."

He was right. "You're wrong."

"Nuh-uh." His lips twitched. "You don't want to wrap your legs around me because that would put you flush against my—hey, stop that!"

She'd found that he was ticklish, and in the nick of time. Within seconds they were both underwater, but at least she was free, and when she resurfaced, Noah was waiting. What ensued then was a good, old-fashioned, rollicking water fight that was broken up at length by Samson's, "Children! Children!"

The water settled some around them as they looked up.

"Bath time," he called. He was lowering a small basket that contained soap and shampoo.

Shaye looked at Noah; Noah looked at Shaye.

"Do you think he's trying to tell us something?" he asked.

"Diplomatically," she answered.

He wrinkled his nose. "Was I that bad?"

"Was *I*?"

"Maybe we canceled each other out."

"So we didn't notice?"

"Yeah." He scowled. "Hell, it's only been three days."

"Three? That's disgusting!"

His eyes widened in accusation. "It has to have been just as long for you."

"Two. Only two, and I've been—"

"Are you going to wash or not?" came the call from above. "We're dying to swim, but we don't want to go in until you get out!"

Shaye looked at Noah in horror. "Is it that bad that they don't want to be near us even in water?"

He laughed and swam toward the basket. "For safety, Shaye. One of us should be on the boat at any given time, and since no one should swim alone, it makes sense to divide it up, two and two." He drew a bright yellow container from the basket and squirted liberal jets of its contents on his arms, hands and neck.

"*Joy?*" she asked, swimming closer.

He tossed her the plastic bottle. "It's one of the few detergents that bubbles in salt water," he explained as he scrubbed his arms, offering proof. "Go on. It does the trick."

She followed his lead and, scissoring steadily with her legs, had soon lathered her arms, shoulders and neck. Noah took the bottle from the basket again and filled his palm, then set to work beneath the waterline. Shaye took her time rinsing her arms.

His eyes grew teasing. "I'm doing my chest. How about you?"

"I'm getting there," she managed, but she was feeling suddenly awkward. She darted a self-conscious glance upward and was relieved to see no sign of Samson.

"You'll need more soap." He tossed his head toward the basket.

She took the bottle, directed a stream of the thick liquid into her hand and replaced the bottle. Then she stared at her palm, wondering how to start.

"Don't turn around," he said. "I want to watch."

"I'm sure."

"Come on. We're in the shadow of the boat. The water's too dark to see anything."

It wasn't what he could see that she feared. It was what he could picture. She knew what *she* was picturing as his shoulders rotated, hands out of sight but very obviously on that broad and virile chest.

"You'd better hurry, Shaye. Samson won't wait forever."

"Okay, okay." With hurried movements, she rubbed her hands together, then thrust them under her suit.

"You could lower the suit. It'd help."

"This is fine." Eyes averted, she soaped her breasts as quickly as she could.

"Look at me while you do that," he commanded softly.

She shot him a glance that was supposed to be quelling, but when her eyes locked with his, she couldn't look away. There was nothing remotely quelling in her gaze then; it mirrored the desire in his. Sudden, startling, explosive. They were separated by a mere arm's length, which, given the expanse of the Caribbean, seemed positively intimate.

Her hands worked over and around her breasts while his hands worked over and around his chest, but it was his fingers she seemed to feel on her sensitive skin, his harder flesh beneath her fingers. When he moved his hands to his lower back, she followed suit and the tingling increased, touching her vertebrae, sizzling down to the base of her spine.

Her lips were parted; her breath rushed past in shallow pants. Her legs continued to scissor, though hypnotically. She was in Noah's thrall, held there by the dark, smoldering charcoal of his eyes and by the force of her own vivid imagination.

The curve of his shoulders indicated that his hands had returned to his front and moved lower. She gulped in a short breath, but her shoulders were also curving, her hands moving forward, then lower.

His eyes held hers, neither mocking nor dropping in an attempt to breach the sea's modest veil. The waves rose and fell around and with them, like a mentor, teaching them the movement, rewarding them with gentle supplementary caresses.

But supplementary caresses were the last things they needed. Shaye felt as though she were vibrating from the inside out, and Noah's muscles were tense, straining for the release that he wouldn't allow himself.

When he closed his eyes for an instant, the spell broke. Two sets of arms joined trembling legs in treading water, and it was a minute more before either of them could speak.

Noah's lips twisted into a self-mocking grin. "You are one hell of a lady to make love with," he said gruffly. "Com'ere."

Shaye gave several rapid shakes of her head.

"I want to do your hair."

"My hair's okay."

He was fishing a bottle of shampoo from the basket when Victoria's voice came over the side. "Aren't you two done *yet?*"

"Be right up," Shaye gasped. She turned to start for the ladder, but a gentle tug on her ponytail brought her right back to Noah. The water worked against her then, denying her the leverage to escape him. And his fingers were already in her hair, easing the thick elastic band from its place. "Please don't, Noah," she begged.

His voice was close to her ear. "Indulge me this, after what you denied me just now."

"Denied you? I didn't deny you a thing!"

"You didn't give me what I *really* wanted. . . ."

She wasn't about to touch that one. So she faced him and held out a hand, palm up. "The shampoo?"

"Right here," he said, pressing his gloppy hand on the top of her head and instantly starting to scrub.

She squeezed her eyes shut. "I'll do it, Noah."

"Too late," he said with an audible grin, then paused. "I've never washed a woman's hair before. Am I doing it right?"

His fingers were everywhere, gathering even the longest strands into the cloud of lather, massaging her scalp, stimulating nerve ends she hadn't known about. Was he doing it right? Was he ever!

She tried to think of something to say, but it was as though his fingers had penetrated her skull and were impeding the workings of her brain. Her eyes were still closed, but in ecstasy now. Her head had fallen back a little as he worked his thumbs along her hairline. She was unaware that her breasts were pushing against his chest, or that her legs had floated around his hips and she was riding him gently in the waves, because those were but small eddies in the overall vortex of pleasure.

His fingers were suddenly still, cupping her head, and his voice was gruff as he pressed his lips to her brow. "Maybe this wasn't such a good idea after all. Better rinse and let me do mine. If our time isn't up, my self-control is."

Shaye opened her eyes then. They widened when she realized how she was holding Noah. "Oh Lord," she whispered and quickly let go. With frantic little movements, she sculled away.

"You're a hussy, Shaye Burke!" Noah taunted. He poured shampoo directly from the bottle onto his head.

She sank underwater and shook her own. When she resurfaced, he was scrubbing his hair, but wore a grin that was
naughty.

"A hussy and a tease!"

"You are a corrupter!" she cried back.

"Me? I was washing your hair! You were the one who tried
to make something more of it!"

Tipping her head to the right to finger-comb water through
her hair, she glared at him. "That's exactly how you're going
to look in ten years, Noah—all white-haired and prune-
faced." She tipped her head to the left and rinsed the long
tresses further. "*No* woman's going to want to look at you
then!"

"So I'd better catch someone now, hmm? Take out an insurance policy?" He submerged, raking the soap from his hair
with his fingers.

"I dare say the premiums would be too high," she called the
minute he'd resurfaced.

"Are you selling?"

"To you? No way!" She headed for the ladder. "You are a
sneaky, no-good . . . seducer of innocent women."

Noah caught her on the second rung, encircling her hips
with one strong arm. He said nothing until she looked down
at him, then asked quietly and without jest, "Are you innocent?"

She could take the question different ways, she knew, but
if she were honest the answer would be the same. No, she
wasn't innocent in what had just happened, because no one
had told her to wrap herself so snugly around him. No, she
hadn't been innocent last night. He hadn't asked her to go
wild in his arms. And she wasn't innocent in that broadest
sense; she'd lost her virginity half a lifetime ago.

Sad eyes conveyed her answer, but she said nothing. Noah
held a frightening power over her already. That power would

surely increase if she confirmed how truly less than innocent she was.

His gaze dropped over her gleaming shoulders and down her bare back to the edge of her suit. His hand slid lower, over the flare of her bottom to her thigh. When he gave her a gentle boost, she climbed the ladder, then crossed the deck to the bow, knowing Noah would remain at the stern to serve as lifeguard to Samson and Victoria.

She needed to be alone. The past weighed too heavily on her to allow for even the most banal of conversation.

SHAYE HAD BEGUN TO REBEL at the age of thirteen, when her father's fierce temper and her mother's conventionalism first crowded in on her budding adolescence. Life to that point had been placid, a sedate cycle revolving around school and church. But she had suddenly developed from a redheaded little girl into an eye-catching teenager, and even if she hadn't seen the change in herself, it would have been impossible for her to mistake the admiring male looks that came her way.

Those looks promised excitement, something she'd never experienced, and she thrived on them, since they compensated for the more dismissing ones she'd received before. Her father was a factory hand, and though he worked hard, the socio-economic class in which the Burkes were trapped was on the lower end of the scale. Donald Burke had been proud to buy the small, two-bedroom cottage in which they lived, because it was on the right side of the tracks, if barely. Unfortunately, the tracks delineated the school districts, which put Shaye and Shannon in classes with far more privileged children.

Gaining the attention of some of the most attractive boys around was a heady experience for Shaye. For the first time she was able to compete with girls she'd envied, girls whose lives where less structured and more frivolous. For the first

time she was able to partake in that frivolity—as the guest of
the very boys those girls covetously eyed.

In theory, Anne Burke wouldn't have objected to the attention her daughter received. She idolized her husband and
was perfectly comfortable with their life, which was not un-
like the one she'd known herself as a child. But she'd seen how
well her sister, Victoria, had done in marrying Arthur Lesser,
and she had no objection to her daughter aiming high.

What she objected to was the fact that Shaye was only
thirteen and that the boys of whom she was enamored were
sixteen and seventeen. They were dangerous ages, ages of
discovery, and Anne Burke didn't want her daughter used.
So she set strict limits on Shaye's social life, and when Shaye
argued, as any normal teenager would, Donald Burke was
there to enforce the law.

Perhaps, Shaye had often mused later, if they'd been a little more flexible she'd have managed—or if she'd been more
manageable, they'd have flexed. But by the time she was fifteen, she felt totally at odds with her parents' conventional-
ity, and her response was to flaunt it in any way she could.
She stole out to a party at Jimmy Danforth's house, when she
was supposedly studying at the library. She cut classes to go
joyriding with Brett Hagen in the Mustang his parents had
given him for his eighteenth birthday. She told her parents she
was baby-sitting, when the baby in question was a dog that
belonged to Alexander Bigelow.

Three days before her sixteenth birthday, she made love
with Ben Parker on the floor of his parents' wine cellar. She'd
known precisely what she was doing and why. She'd given
her innocence to Ben because it was fun and exciting and a
little bit dangerous—and because it was the last thing her
parents wanted her to do.

She was her own person, she'd decided. If her parents were
happy with their lives, that was fine, but she resented the

dogma of hard work and self-restraint that they imposed on her. Discovering that she could have a wonderful time—and get away with it—was self-perpetuating.

She played her way through high school. Reasonably bright, she maintained a B average without much effort—a good thing, since she didn't have much time to spare from her social life. Fights with her parents were long and drawn out, until true communication became almost nonexistent. That didn't bother Shaye. She knew what she wanted to do, and she did it. She applied to NYU, was accepted on scholarship, and finally escaped her parents' watchful eyes.

New York was as much fun as she'd hoped. She liked her classes, but she liked even more the freedom she had and the people she met. And she adored Victoria, whom she saw regularly. In hindsight, Shaye knew that keeping in such close touch with her aunt represented a need for family ties. At the time she only knew Victoria understood her as her parents never had.

Victoria was as different from her sister, Anne, as night from day. While Anne chose to take the more traveled highways through life, Victoria took the back roads that led to greater beauty and pleasure. The one thing they shared was their devotion to their husbands, but since each had married a man to suit her tastes, their differences had grown more marked as time went on.

Shaye identified with Victoria. It wasn't that she yearned to be wealthy; wealth, or the lack of it, had never played as prominently in her mind as had adventure. But Victoria *did* things. She acted on her impulses, rather than putting them off for a day far in the future. And if she subtly cautioned Shaye to exercise moderation, Shaye put it down to the loyalty Victoria felt toward Anne.

Despite Victoria's subtle words of caution, Shaye had a ball. In February of her freshman year she hitchhiked with

Graham Hauk to New Orleans for Mardi Gras. That summer she took a house in Provincetown with five friends, all of whom were working, as she was, in local restaurants. Much of her sophomore year was spent at the off-campus apartment of Josh Milgram, her latest love and a graduate student of philosophy, who had a group of ever-present and fascinating, if bizarre, friends.

She spent the summer before her junior year selling computer equipment in Washington. She'd secured the job principally on her interview, during which she'd demonstrated both an aptitude for handling the equipment and an aptitude for selling herself. She loved Washington. Sharing an apartment with two friends from school, she had regular working hours, which left plenty of time for play.

It was during that summer that Shannon joined her, and Shaye couldn't have been more delighted. She'd always felt that Shannon was being stifled at home. More than once she'd urged her sister to break out, but it was only by dint of a summer-school program held at American University for high school students that Shannon made it.

Proud of her sister, Shaye introduced her to all her friends. At summer's end, she sent Shannon back home reasonably assured that she was awakened to the pleasures of life.

Shaye whizzed through her junior year seeing Tom, Peter and Gene, but the real fun came in her senior year when she met André. André—né Andrew, but he'd decided that that name was too plebeian—was a perpetual student of art. He had a small garret in Soho, where Shaye spent most of her time, and a revolving group of friends and followers who offered never-ending novelty. André and Shaye were a couple, but in the loosest sense of the word. André was far from possessive, and Shaye was far from committed. She adored André for his eccentricity; his painting was as eclectic as his lovemaking. But she adored Christopher's brashness and Jamal's wild imagination and Stefan's incredible irreverence.

She was treading a fine line in her personal life, though at the time she didn't see it. Graduating from college, she took a position in the computer department of an insurance company, and if her friends teased her about such a staid job, she merely laughed, took a puff of the nearest pipe and did something totally outrageous to show where her heart lay.

She was one year out of college and living at the garret with André and his friends when the folly of her life-style hit home.

"Fräulein?"

Shaye's head shot up, her thoughts boomeranging back to the present. Her eyes focused on Samson, who was wearing a black tuxedo jacket with tails and, beneath it, a white apron tied at the waist and falling to mid-calf.

"Darf ich Sie bitten, an unserem Dinner *teilzunehmen? Wir sind bereit; bitte sagen Sie nicht nein."*

It was a minute before comprehension came. She didn't speak German, but a pattern was emerging, reinforced by the sight of Victoria and Noah already settling at the table on the other end of the deck.

She didn't know how long she'd been sitting so lost in thought—an hour, perhaps two—but she was grateful for the rescue. Smiling, she took the hand Samson graciously offered, realizing only after she'd risen that she was still wearing her bathing suit.

"Let me change first," she said softly.

"You don't need to."

But she'd be asking for trouble from Noah if she appeared at dinner so minimally covered. "I'll be quick."

Hurrying below, she discarded the suit and drew on a one-piece shorts outfit. She'd reached the companionway before realizing that her hair was still down. Deciding that it was too late to pin it up, she finger-combed it back from her face and continued to the deck.

Dinner was sauerbraten, red cabbage and strudel. It was accompanied by a sturdy red Ingelheimer whose mildly sedative effect helped Shaye handle both the lingering shadow of her reminiscing and Noah's very large, very virile and observant presence.

Actually, he behaved himself admirably, or so he decided. He didn't make any comments about Shaye's free-flowing hair, though he was dying to. Even more, he was dying to touch it. Clean and shining, it seemed thicker than ever, as though its life had been released by the sea and the breeze. Nor did he comment on her smile, which was coming more frequently. He wondered if it was the wine, or whether the afternoon swim had eased a certain tension from her. Somehow he doubted the latter, after the words they'd exchanged in the water. But she'd spent a good long time since then at the bow, and he wondered if what she'd been thinking about was responsible for the softening of her mood.

He'd watched her but she hadn't known it. She'd been lost in a world of her own. Even now, sitting over the last of the wine, she faded in and out from time to time. During those "out" phases her expression was mellow, vaguely sad—as it had been on the rope ladder when he'd asked about her innocence.

He was more curious about her than ever, but he could bide his time. Sunset was upon them. Soon it would be dark. Perhaps if her mellow mood continued, he'd be able to pry some information from her without a fight.

After dinner Shaye returned to her perch at the bow. She took a cushion with her, and though she'd fetched a book, she didn't bother to open it. Instead, she propped herself comfortably and studied the sky.

To the west were the deepening orange colors of the waning day, above that the purples of early night. As she watched, the purples spread and darkened, until the last of the sun's rays had been swallowed up.

She took one deep breath, then another. Her body felt clean and relaxed, and if her mind wasn't in quite that perfect a state, it was close. There were things to be considered, but not now, not when the Caribbean night was so beautiful.

Victoria was with Samson at the helm. They clearly enjoyed each other, and, deep down inside, Shaye was pleased. Samson was an interesting man. He had the style and spirit to make Victoria's trip an adventure even without the treasure no one had spoken of yet.

Shifting herself and the cushion so that she was lying down, she crossed her ankles, folded her hands on her middle and closed her eyes. So different from home, she mused. She couldn't remember the last time she'd lain down like this and just . . . listened. What was there to listen to in her Philadelphia apartment? Traffic? The siren of a police car or an ambulance? Peals of laughter from a party at one of the other apartments?

None of that here. Just the rhythmic thrust of the waves against the hull and the periodic flap of a sail. There was something to be said for going on a treasure hunt after all.

Her brow creased lightly. Noah had said that there were different types of treasures to be sought, and he was right. He seemed to be right about a lot of things. She had to define the treasure *she* was seeking. Was it a job well done in Philadelphia? Career advancement? Perhaps movement to a broader, more prestigious position?

After all she'd thought about that afternoon, she had to smile. Her life now was the antithesis of what it had been seven, eight, nine years before. If someone had told her then what she'd be doing in subsequent years, she'd have thought him mad.

But even back then, without conscious planning, she'd made provisions for a more stable life. She'd completed her education and had established herself in a lucrative field. Had her subconscious known something?

The question was whether the life she now had would stand her in good stead for the next thirty years. If so, if she was as self-contained and complete a being as she'd thought, why did Noah VanBaar make her ache? Did her subconscious know something else?

Eyes still closed, she grew alert. He was here now. She hadn't heard him approach, but she knew he was near. There was something hovering, newly coagulating in her mind...a sense of familiarity, a scent. Noah. Smelling of the sun and the sea, of musk and man.

She opened her eyes and met his curious gaze. He was squatting an arm's length away, a dimly-glowing lantern hanging from his fingers.

"I wasn't sure if you were sleeping."

"I wasn't."

"You've been lying here a long time."

And still she didn't move; she felt too comfortable. "It's peaceful." Was that a hint that he should leave? She was trying to decide if she wanted him to when he reached up, hooked the lantern on the bowsprit, then sat down and stretched out his legs. She'd known he wouldn't ask to join her; that wasn't his style. In a way she was glad he hadn't. She'd been spared having to make the choice.

Resting his head back, he sighed. "We're almost halfway there. From the looks of the clouds in the east, we may get a push."

"Clouds?" She peered eastward. "I don't see a thing."

"Mmm. No moon, no stars."

"Oh, dear. A storm?"

He shrugged. "Who knows? Maybe rain, maybe wind, maybe nothing. Storm clouds can veer off. They can dissipate. Weather at sea is fickle."

Sliding an arm behind her head, she studied him. "You must sail a lot."

"Not so much now. I used to though. Samson got me hooked when I was a kid. I spent several summers crewing on windjammers off the coast of Maine."

"Sounds like fun."

"It was. I love the ocean, especially when it's wild. I could sit for hours and watch the waves thrash about."

"You should have a place on the coast, rather than in Vermont."

"Nah. Watching the ocean in a storm is inspirational, not restful. When I leave the city on weekends, I need rest."

"The city—New York?"

He nodded.

"What do you do?"

"Are you sure you want to know?"

"Why wouldn't I?"

"Because knowing about me will bring us closer, and I had the impression that you wanted to stay as far from me as possible."

"True. But tell me anyway."

"Why?"

"Because I'm curious."

He considered that. "I suppose it's as good a reason as any. Of course," he tilted his head and his voice turned whimsical, "it would be nicer if you'd said that you've changed your mind about staying away, or that you want to know about the man who's swept you off your feet, or—" his voice dropped "—that you're as interested in exploring my mind as you are in exploring my body."

Her skin tingled and she was grateful that the lantern was more a beacon to other ships than an illuminator of theirs. The dark was her protector, when she felt oddly exposed. "Just tell me," she grumbled, then added a taunting, "unless you have something to hide."

That was all Noah needed to hear. "I'm a political pollster."

"A political—"

"Pollster. When a guy decides to make a run for political office, he hires me to keep tabs on his status among the electorate."

"Interesting," she said and meant it.

"I think so. Actually, I started out doing only polling, but the business has evolved into something akin to public relations."

"In what sense?"

Encouraged that she wanted to hear more, Noah explained. "John Doe comes to me and says that he's running for office. I do my research, ferreting out his opponent's strengths and weaknesses, plus the characteristics of the constituency. Between us we determine the image we want to project, the kind of image that will go across with the voters—"

"But isn't that cheating? If you tailor-make the candidate to the voters, what about issues? Isn't John Doe compromising himself?"

"Not at all. He doesn't alter his stand; he merely alters the way that stand is put across. One or another of his positions may be more popular among the voters, so we focus on those and push the others into the background. The key is to get the man elected, at which point he can bring other issues forward."

"Clever, if a little devious."

"That's the way the game is played. His opponent does it; why shouldn't he? It's most useful on matters that have little to do with the issues."

"Such as...?"

"Age. Marital status. Religion, ethnic background, prior political experience. Again, it's a question of playing something up or down, depending on the bias of the voters."

Shaye frowned. "Sounds to me like there's a very fine line between your job and an ad agency's."

"Sure is, and that's who takes over from me. Ad agencies, media consultants—they're the ones who put together the specifics of the campaign itself."

"And your job is done at that point?"

He shook his head. "We keep polling right up to, sometimes beyond, the campaign. Obviously, some candidates have more money to pay for our services than others. By the same token, some political offices require more ongoing work than others."

She could easily guess which offices those would be and was duly impressed. "I suppose that's good for you. Otherwise you'd have a pretty seasonal job."

"Seasonal it isn't," he drawled. "I use the word 'political' in the broadest sense. We do polling for lobbyists, for public interest groups, for hospitals and real estate developers and educational institutions."

"When you say 'we,' who do you mean?"

"I have a full-time staff of ninety people, with several hundred part-timers on call."

"But you're the leader?"

"It's my baby, yes."

"You started it from scratch?"

"Planted the seed and nurtured it," he said with an inflection of intimacy that made her blush. He didn't follow up, though, but leaned forward and rubbed his back before returning to his original position.

"You must feel proud."

"I do."

"There must be a lot of pressure."

He nodded.

"But it's rewarding?"

"Very." He sat forward again and flexed his back muscles, then grumbled crossly, "This boat leaves much to be desired by way of comfort. I've never heard of a boat with a deck this size and no deck chairs."

She was hard put not to laugh, clearly recalling the discussion she'd had with Victoria when they'd first boarded the sloop, a discussion Noah had overheard and mocked. "You don't like the *Golden Echo*?" she asked sweetly.

He heard the jibe in her tone and couldn't let it go unanswered. In the blink of an eye, he'd closed the distance between them, displaced her from the cushion and drawn her to him so that her back was against his chest.

6

SHAYE TRIED TO WIGGLE AWAY, but Noah hooked his legs around hers. When she continued to squirm, he made a low, sexy sound. "Ooh, that feels good. A little more pressure . . . there . . . lower."

Abruptly she went still. "This is not a good idea, Noah."

"My back sure feels a hell of a lot better."

"Mine doesn't."

"That's because you've got a rod up it—" He caught himself and backed off. "Uh, no, that came out the wrong way. What I meant was that you've stiffened up. If you relax and let me cushion you, you'll be as comfortable as you were before."

That was what Shaye feared, but the temptation was great. It was a peaceful night and she'd been interested in what he'd been saying. Would it hurt to relax a little?

"Better," he said with a sigh when he felt her body soften to his. Though his legs fell away, his arms remained loosely around her waist. He'd thrown on a shirt after dinner, but it was unbuttoned. Her hair formed a thick pillow on his chest, with wayward strands teasing his throat and chin.

Having made the decision to stay in his arms, Shaye was surprisingly content. "Have you ever been married?"

"Where did that come from?"

"I was thinking about your work. You said there was pressure, and I assume the hours are long. I was curious."

Curious, again. Okay. "No. I've never been married."

"Do you dislike women?"

"Where did *that* come from?"

"One of the first things you said you didn't like about me was that I was a woman."

"Ah. That was because I hadn't known there were going to be women along on this trip until a few minutes before you and your aunt arrived."

"And it bothered you?"

"At the time."

"Why?"

"Because I wanted to get away from it all. Before Samson drafted me I'd planned to spend two weeks alone in Normandy."

"Normandy." She slid her head sideways and looked up at him. "A château?"

"A small one."

She righted her head. "Small one, big one...it sounds lovely."

"It would have been, but this isn't so bad."

"Would you have done anything differently if Victoria and I hadn't been along?"

"A few things."

"Like...?"

"Shaving. I wouldn't have bothered."

"You don't have to shave for our sakes. Be my guest. Grow a beard."

He'd been hoping she'd thank him; after all, stubble looked grubby, and then there was the matter of kissing. But she wouldn't consider that. Not Shaye.

"I don't want to grow a beard," he grumbled. "I just didn't want to have to shave unless I felt like it."

"So don't." She paused. "What else would you have done if we weren't along?"

"Swam in the nude. Sunbathed in the nude. *Sailed* in the nude," he added just for spite.

Forgetting that she was supposed to be prissy, she grinned. "That would be a sight."

"Oh God, are we onto that again? Why is it that everyone's always insulting my manhood?"

She shaped her hands to his wrists and gave a squeeze. "I'm just teasing... though I don't believe I've ever seen a naked pirate before."

"This is not a pirate ship," was his arch response.

"Then, a naked patriot."

"Have you ever seen any man naked?"

Her grin was hidden. He should only know. "I saw *American Gigolo*. There were some pretty explicit scenes."

He tightened his arms in mock punishment. "A real man. In the flesh. Have you ever seen one up close and all over?"

"I walked in on my father once when I was little."

He sighed. "I'm not talking about—"

"I've learned to keep my eyes shut since then."

Which told him absolutely nothing. So he put that particular subject on hold and tried one he thought she'd find simpler to answer. "What kind of work do you do?"

She hesitated, then echoed his own earlier question. "Are you sure you want to know?"

"Why wouldn't I?"

"Because you won't like the answer."

"Why not?"

"Because it fits my personality to a tee."

"You're the headmistress of an all-girls school?"

"Nope."

"A warden at a penitentiary?"

She shook her head.

"I give up. What do you do?"

Again she hesitated, then confessed, "I work with computers."

"That figures."

"I told you you wouldn't like it."

"I didn't say I didn't like it, just that it figures. You work with machines. Very structured and controlled." He lowered his voice. "Do they turn you on?"

"Shows how much you know about computers. Noah, you have to turn *them* on or they don't do a thing."

She was teasing, and he loved it. He wasn't quite sure why she was in such good humor, but he wasn't about to upset the applecart by saying something lewd. "Once you turn them on, what do you do with them?"

"Same thing you do. Program them to store information and spit it back up on command."

"Your command?"

"Or one of my assistants'."

"Then you're the one in charge?"

"Of the department, yes."

"Where is the department?"

"In a law firm."

"A law firm in Philadelphia." Her head bobbed against his chest. He loved that, too—the undulating silk of her hair against his bare skin. "So—" he cleared his throat "—what kind of information are we dealing with here?"

"Client files, financial projections, accounts receivable, attorney profitability reports, balance sheets." She reeled them off, pausing only at the end for a breath. "Increasingly we're using the computers for the preparation of documents. And we're plugged into LEXIS."

"What's LEXIS?"

"A national computer program for research. By typing certain codes into the computer, our lawyers can find cases or law review articles that they need for briefs. It saves hours of work in the library."

"I'm impressed."

She swiveled and met his gaze. "By LEXIS?"

"By you. You really know what you're talking about."

"You didn't think I would?"

"It's not that," he said. "But you sound so . . . so on top of the whole thing."

"How do you think I got where I am?"

"I don't know. How did you?" His voice dropped to a teasing drawl. He couldn't resist; she was so damned sexy peering up at him that way. "Did you wow all those computer guys with your body?"

She stared at him for a minute, then faced forward. "Exactly."

"Come on," he soothed, brushing her ear with his mouth. "I know you wouldn't do that. Tell me how you got hooked up with computers."

"I took computer courses in college."

"And that was it? A few courses and, pow, you're the head of a department?"

"Of course not. I worked summers, then worked after graduation, and by the time the opening came at the law firm, I had the credentials and was there."

"How large is the firm?"

"Seventy-five lawyers."

"General practice?"

"Corporate."

"Ahh. Big money-getters."

"Lucky for me. If they weren't, they'd never be able to support a computer department the size of ours, and my job would be neither as interesting nor as challenging."

"Are they nice?"

"The lawyers? Some I like better than others."

"Do they treat you well?"

"I'm not complaining."

"But you do love your work."

"Yes."

"Any long-range ambitions?"

"I don't know. I'm thinking about that. I've risen pretty fast in a field that's steadily changing."

"Personnel-wise?"

"Equipment-wise. Personnel-wise, too, I guess. A lot of people jumped on the bandwagon when computers first got big, but time has weeded out the men from the boys."

"Or the women from the girls."

"Mmm."

He nudged her foot with his. "What about marriage? Or pregnancy? Does that weed out the women from the girls?"

"Not as much as it used to. The firm is generous when it comes to maternity leave. Many of the women, lawyers included, have taken time off, then returned. In my department, word processing is done round the clock. Women can choose their shifts to accommodate child-care arrangements."

"Is that what you'll do?"

"I hadn't thought I was pregnant," she remarked blithely.

"Do you want to be?"

"I like what I'm doing now."

"Cuddling?"

"Heading the computer department."

He bent his knees and brought his legs in closer. "But someday. Do you want to have kids?"

"I haven't really thought about it."

"Come on. Every woman thinks about it."

"I've been too busy."

"To do it?"

"To think about doing it."

He dipped his head, bringing his lips into warm intimacy with her cheek. "I'll give you a baby."

She shifted, turning onto her side so she could better see his expression. "You're crazy, do you know that?"

"Not really."

"Give me a baby—why in the world would you say something like that? In case you don't know it, a baby takes after both its parents. I've been bugging you since I stepped foot on this sloop. How would you like to have a baby that bugged you from the day it was born?"

He shrugged. "There's bugging, and there's bugging." Her hand was using his chest for leverage; he covered it with his own. "You have certain qualities that I'd want in a child of mine."

"Like what?"

It was a minute before he answered. "Beauty."

She shot a quick glance skyward. "Spare me."

"Intelligence."

"That's a given." She tipped up her chin. "What else?" When he was quiet, she gave him a lopsided grin. "Run out of things already?"

It wasn't that he'd run out, just that he was having trouble concentrating. She was so soft in his arms, her face so pert as it tilted toward his, her legs smooth as they tangled with his, her hip firm as it pressed his groin.

"There's . . . there's spunk."

"Spunk?"

"Sure. Seven times out of ten you have answers for my jibes."

"Only seven?"

Almost imperceptibly, he moved her hand on his chest. He closed his eyes for a minute and swallowed hard. "Maybe eight."

"But I'm stern-faced and prissy," she said, shifting slightly. "Is that what you want your children to inherit?"

He'd closed his eyes again, and when he opened them, he was smiling ever so gently, ever so wryly, and his warning came ever so softly. "You're playing with fire."

"I . . . what?"

"Your legs brush mine, your hair torments me." His voice began to sizzle. "You move those hips and I'm on fire, and your hand on my skin gives me such pleasure. . . . Can't you feel what's happening?"

Her stunned eyes dropped to her hand. It was partially covered by his, but her fingers were buried in the soft, curling hairs on his chest. As she watched, they began to tingle, then throb above the beat of his heart.

"A little to your right," he whispered huskily. "Move them."

She swallowed. Her fingers straightened and inched forward until a single digit came to rest atop a clearly erect nipple.

He moaned and moved his hips.

Her eyes flew to his face.

"Shocked?" he asked thickly. "Didn't you know? Am I the only one suffering?"

"I . . . we were talking . . . I was comfortable." The words seemed feeble, but they were the truth. She couldn't remember when she'd ever been with a man this way, just talking, enjoying the physical closeness for something other than sex. "I'm sorry. . . ."

But she didn't move away. Her senses were awakening to him with incredible speed. All the little things that had hovered just beyond sexual awareness—the sole of his foot against her instep, the brush of his hair-spattered legs against her calves and thighs, the solidity of his flesh beneath her hand, his enveloping male scent, the cradle of his body, the swelling virility between his legs—all came into vivid focus. And his voice, his voice, honing her awareness like scintillating sand . . .

"I'd like to make love to you, Shaye. I'd like to open that little thing you're wearing and touch you all over, taste you all over. I think I could bury myself in your body and never miss the world again. Would you let me do that?"

The rising breeze cooled her face, but she could barely breathe, much less think. "I . . . we can't."

"We can." He had one arm across her back in support while his hand caressed her hip. The other hand tipped up her face. "Kiss me, Shaye. Now."

Say no. Push him away. Tell him you don't want this. She had the answers but no motivation, and when his mouth closed over hers, she could do nothing but savor its purposeful movement. Caressing, sucking, stroking—he was a man who kissed long and well. He was also a man who demanded a response.

"Open your mouth," he ordered in an uncompromising growl. "Do it the way I like it."

Shaye wasn't quite sure how he liked it, but the break in his kiss had left her hungry. This time when he seized them, her lips were parted. As they had the night before, they erupted into a fever against his, building the heat so high that she had to use her tongue as a coolant. But that didn't work, either, because Noah's own response increased the friction. Her breath came quickly, and her entire body was trembling by the time he dragged his lips away.

"Ahh, you do it right," he said on a groan.

Gasping softly, she pressed her forehead to his jaw. She felt his hand on her neck, but she was too weak to object, and in a second that hand was inside her blouse, taking the full weight of her breast. Her small cry was lifted and carried away by the wind.

"This is what I want," he whispered. His long fingers kneaded her, then drew a large arc on her engorged flesh. The top snap of her blouse released at the pressure of his wrist, but she barely heard it. His palm was passing over her nipple once, then again, and his fingers settled more broadly when his thumb took command.

"Look at me, Shaye."

Through passion-glazed eyes, she looked.

His voice was a rasping whisper. "This is what I'd do for starters." As he held her gaze, he dragged his thumb directly across her turgid nipple. He repeated the motion. "Do you feel it inside?"

"Oh yes," she whispered back. The thrumming still echoed in her core. Her legs stirred restlessly. "Do it again."

A tiny whimper came from the back of her throat when he did, but then he was whispering again. "I'd touch the other one like that, too. And then I'd take it in my mouth. . . ." Another snap popped and he lowered his head. She took handfuls of his hair and held on when his thumb was replaced by the heat of his mouth, the wetness of his tongue, the gentle but volatile raking of his teeth.

Nothing had ever felt so exciting and so right. Shaye had spent the past six years of her life denying that the two—exciting and right—could be compatible, but she couldn't deny what she felt now. As his mouth drew her swelling breast deeper and deeper into its hot, wet hold, she knew both peace and yearning. She wanted him to tell her what he'd do next, and she wanted him to do it. She ached to do all kinds of wild things in return. And still there was that sense of rightness, and it confused her.

"Noah . . . Noah, Samson . . ."

"Can't see. Shh."

She wanted, but she didn't. The feel of Noah's mouth firmly latched to her burning flesh was a dangerous Eden. She didn't trust herself and her judgement of rightness, and she couldn't trust Noah to understand what she felt. She was in deep water and sinking fast. If she didn't haul herself up soon, she'd be lost.

Tugging at his hair, she pulled him away with a moan. "We have to stop."

"Samson's way back at the stern," Noah argued hoarsely. "The sails are between us and him, and it's dark."

But Shaye was already sliding from his lap. He watched her scramble against the bow, clutching the lapels of her blouse with one hand, holding her middle with the other. His body was throbbing and his breathing unsteady. He hiked his knees up and wrapped his arms around them. "It's not just Samson," he stated.

"No."

"Is it me?"

"No."

"Then it's you."

She said nothing, just continued to look at him. The wind had picked up, blowing her hair around her face. She was almost grateful for the shield.

Her insides were in knots. She felt as though she'd been standing on the brink of either utter glory or total disaster—only she didn't know which. If he took her back in his arms, coaxed the least bit, pushed the least bit, she'd give in. Her nipple was still damp where he'd suckled; both breasts—her entire body—tingled. She'd never in her life felt as strong a craving for more, and she didn't understand why.

But common sense cried for self-control. Self-control! Was it so much to ask? Shaye wondered. When she'd been younger, she'd thought that by doing her own thing when and where she wanted, she was controlling her life. In fact, the opposite had been the case. For years she'd been out of control, acting irresponsibly with little thought for the consequences of her actions.

Now she was older and wiser. Responsibility had closed in on her, weighing her down at times, uplifting her at others. Perhaps it was an obsession, but self-control had been a passion in and of itself.

"What is it, Shaye?" Noah asked. "You're not an eighteen-year-old virgin."

She'd never been an eighteen-year-old virgin, and that was part of the problem. She'd given in too soon, too fast, too far.

"Have you been hurt . . . abused?"

"No!"

"But you're afraid."

"I just want to stop."

"You're afraid."

"Think what you will."

"But it doesn't make sense!" he burst out in frustration. "One minute you want me, the next you don't."

"I know."

"Well? Are you going to explain?" The demands of his body had died. He stretched out his legs in a show of indolence he was far from feeling. The wind was whipping at his shirt, but when he folded his arms over his chest, it was more because he felt exposed to Shaye's whims than to those of the weather. He wasn't used to the feeling of exposure and didn't like it.

"I can't explain. It's just . . . just me."

"Have you ever been involved with a man?"

"I've never been in love."

"That wasn't the question. Have you ever had a relationship with a man?"

"Certainly—just as you have."

"Sexually. Have you ever been involved sexually with a man?"

"You pointed out—" she began, then repeated herself in a voice loud enough to breach the wind "—you pointed out that I'm not an eighteen-year-old virgin."

He sighed, but the sound was instantly whisked away. "Shaye, you know what I'm getting at."

"I've been involved with many men, but never deeply," she blurted out, then wondered why she had. At the time she'd thought herself deeply involved with Josh...or André...or Christopher. But "deep" meant something very different now. It was almost...almost the way she was beginning to think herself involved with Noah, and that stunned her.

"Have you ever lived with a man?"

It was a minute before she could answer. "I, uh, lived in a kind of communal setup for a while," she hedged, and even that was pushing it a little. The garret had been André's; the others had simply crashed there for a time. She'd spent seven months with Josh, who'd eventually run off—with her blessing—to follow the Maharishi. She'd lived with other men for brief periods; she'd quickly gotten restless.

"Communal setups can mean either constant sex or no sex at all. Which was it?"

"I'm prissy. Which do you think?"

"I'm beginning to think this prissy bit is a cop-out. I'm beginning to think you're not one bit prissy. At least, that's what your fiery little body leads me to suspect."

She shrugged.

"Damn it, don't do that," he snapped. The sloop seemed to echo his frustration with a sudden roll. "I'm trying to get information. Shrugging tells me nothing."

"I don't like being the butt of your polling."

He rubbed the tight muscles at the back of his neck. "Was it that obvious?"

"Now that I know what you do for a living, yes."

The flapping of canvas high above suddenly grabbed their attention. Noah sprang to his feet. "It's about to rain. Do you have a slicker?"

Shaye, too, had risen. She'd snapped up her blouse and was holding her hair off her face with both hands. "A poncho." She swayed toward the bulwark when the boat took a lunge.

"Better get it," he said as he started toward the stern. She was right behind him. "Better still, get below. This deck in a storm is no place for a woman."

Shaye was about to make a derisive retort when Noah started shouting to Samson. And at the moment the first large drops of rain hit the deck. Having no desire to get drenched, she made straight for the companionway.

For several hours, she remained in the salon with Victoria while the *Golden Echo* bucked the waves with something less than grace. The men had run below in turns to get rain gear, and Shaye's repeated offers of help had been refused. She noticed that Victoria wasn't offering. In fact, Victoria was very quiet.

"Are you feeling all right?"

"I'm fine," Victoria said softly. "Or I will be once the wind dies down."

"That could be hours from now."

The expression on Victoria's face would have been priceless if she hadn't been so pale. "Don't remind me."

"Why don't you lie down in the cabin?"

"I'm afraid that might be worse." She scowled. "This tub isn't the best thing to be on in weather like this."

"So it's a tub now, is it?" Shaye said with a teasing smile. "You didn't think so before."

"Before I wasn't being jostled. And the portholes were open then." Victoria fanned herself. "It's hot as Hades here."

"Would you rather the waves poured in?"

"No, no. Not that."

"Are you scared?"

"Are you?"

Shaye was, a little. But the storm was a diversion. It gave her something to think about besides Noah and herself. Even now, with little effort, she could feel his arms around her and his tongue on her breast. She felt the same yearning she had then, the same confusion, the same fear. She'd come so close to giving in. . . .

But she couldn't think about that. There was the storm to consider, one danger exchanged for another. She did trust that Samson and Noah knew what they were doing. She wondered if they were frightened—but didn't really want to know.

So she pasted a crooked grin on her face and said to Victoria, "I'm sure we'll pull through fine. Look at the experience as exciting. It's not everyone who gets tossed over the high seas in an ancient colonial sloop."

"Cute," Victoria said, then gingerly pushed herself from the sofa. "On second thought, I will lie down."

Concerned, Shaye started out of her chair. "Can I do anything to help?"

But Victoria pressed her shoulder down as she passed. "If death is imminent, I'll call."

SHAYE DIDN'T WAIT for the call. She checked on Victoria every few minutes, trying to talk her out of her preoccupation with her insides. But with each visit, Victoria felt less like talking. By the third visit, she'd lost the contents of her stomach and was looking like death warmed over.

"Let me get you something."

Victoria moaned. "Leave me be."

"But I feel helpless."

"It'll pass."

"My helplessness?"

"My seasickness."

"What about my guilt?" Shaye asked in a meek stab at humor. "I was the one who joked about getting violently seasick."

"Tss. You're making it worse."

"Samson said he had medicine."

"Don't bother Samson. He has enough on his hands."

Shaye rose from the bed. "I'm getting his medicine."

"They'll think I'm a sissy."

"God forbid."

"Shaye, I'm fine—"

"You will be," she said as she left the cabin. Shimmying into her poncho, she climbed the companionway. She paused only to raise her hood and duck her head in preparation for the rain before pushing open the hatch. The wind instantly whipped the hood back and her hair was soaked before she'd reached the helm, where Samson stood wearing bright yellow oilskins and a sou'wester, looking for all the world like a seasoned Gloucester fisherman.

"Whatcha doin' up heah, geul?" he yelled in an accent to match.

The rain was coming down in sheets while the wind whipped everything in sight, but still Shaye laughed. His role playing conveyed a confidence that was contagious. "You're too much, Samson!"

"Best enjoy ev'ry minute!" he declared in a voice that challenged the storm.

Shaye tugged up her hood to deflect the rain from her face while she looked around. The sea was a mass of whitecaps. The jibs were down, the mainsail reefed. In essence, Samson was doing little more than holding the keel steady while they rode out the storm.

"Has Noah gone overboard?" she yelled.

"Not likely!"

She was about to ask where he was when the boat heaved
and veered to port. Steadying herself as best she could, she
shouted, "Are we in danger?"

He straightened the wheel and shouted back, "Nope!"

"How long do you think it'll keep up?"

"Mebbe an hour. Mebbe five."

"Victoria won't be terribly pleased to hear that."

"She'll prob'ly be hopin' it las' ten," he roared with an ap-
preciative smile.

"I don't think so, Samson. She's sick!"

While the storm didn't faze him, that bit of news did. For
the first time, he seemed concerned. The accent vanished.
"Her stomach's acting up?"

Shaye nodded vigorously. "You said something about
medicine?"

"In the locker by the galley. Noah may have it, though."

"Where *is* Noah?"

"In bed."

"What's he doing in bed when—oh, no, he's sick?"

"And not pleased about it at all! He wanted to stay on deck,
but when he started to reel on his feet, I ordered him down."

Shaye had no way of knowing that the same concern she'd
seen on Samson's face moments before now registered on her
own. Noah sick? He was so large, so strong. She couldn't
picture him being brought down by anything, much less *mal
de mer*.

Actually, though, the more she thought about it, the more
she saw a touch of humor in it. Or poetic justice.

"I didn't see him come in," she said more to herself than to
Samson. "It must have been while I was with Victoria."

At the reminder of her aunt, she turned quickly back to the
hatch. Once below, she peeled off the soaking poncho and
checked the locker for Samson's medicine. It was there. Either

Noah wasn't all that sick or he was too proud to take anything.

Victoria wasn't too proud. When Shaye lifted her head and pressed the pill between her lips, she sipped enough water to get it down, then sank weakly back to the pillow. Pill bottle in hand, Shaye returned to the locker. She paused before opening it, though, eyes moving helplessly toward the captain's quarters. Then, without asking herself why or to what end, she took the few steps necessary and quietly opened the door.

A trail of sodden clothes led to the bed, and on that bed lay Noah. He was sprawled on his stomach atop the bare sheets, one arm thrown over his head. The faint glow from the lamp showed the sheen of sweat that covered his body. He was naked.

Feeling not humor but a well of compassion that she'd never have dreamed she'd feel for the man, she quietly approached and knelt down by the bed. "Noah?" she asked softly.

He moaned and turned his face away.

"Have you taken something?"

He grunted.

Compassion turned to tenderness. She reached out and stroked his hair. It was wet from the rain, but his neck was clammy. "Victoria's sick. I just gave her some of Samson's medicine. If I get water, will you take some, too?"

He groaned. "Let me die in peace."

"You're not going to die."

He made a throaty sound of agreement. "I won't be so lucky."

"If you die, who'll be left to give me a hard time?"

There was a short silence from Noah, then a terse, "Get the pill."

Shaye brought water and held his head while he managed to swallow the pill. Then she sponged his back with a damp cloth.

"It's not helping," he mumbled. Though his head was turned her way, his eyes remained closed.

"Give it time."

"I haven't got time. I'm already in hell."

"Serves you right for living the life of a sinner."

He moaned, then grumbled, "What would you know about the life of a sinner?"

"You'd be surprised," she answered lightly, continuing to bathe him.

At length he dragged open an eye. "Why aren't *you* sick?"

"I'm just not."

"Are you scared."

"No."

"You should be. We're about to be swallowed by a great white whale."

"Does delirium come with seasickness?"

He gave up the effort of keeping that one eye open, pulled the pillow between his chest and the sheet and moaned again.

"Does that help?" she asked.

"What?"

"Moaning."

"Yes." A minute later he turned onto his side and curled into a ball, with the pillow pressed to his stomach. "God, I feel awful."

He looked it. His face was an ashen contrast to his dark hair, and tight lines rimmed his nose and mouth.

"Are you going to be sick?" she said.

"I *am* sick."

"Are you going to throw up?"

"Already have. Twice."

"That should have helped."

He grunted.

"It's really a shame. After Samson went to such efforts with the sauerbraten—"

"Shut up, Shaye," he gasped, then gave another moan.

"The storm should be over sometime tomorrow."

"If you can't say something nice . . ."

"I thought the storm was pretty exciting. I've never seen waves quite like that."

This time his moan had more feeling. Shaye said nothing more as she smoothed the cloth over his skin a final time. Then, brushing the damp hair from his brow, she asked, "Will you be okay?"

"Fine."

"I should get back to Victoria."

"Go."

"Can I check on you later?"

"Only if you're into autopsies."

She smiled. He was the fallen warrior, but there was something endearing about him. "I'll steel myself," she said, then quietly rose from his bedside and left the cabin.

She didn't steel herself for an autopsy, of course. She checked on Victoria, who'd settled some, then went to sleep to dream dreams of a long-legged, lean-hipped man whose body had to be the most beautiful she'd ever seen in her life.

7

THE STORM HAD DIED by morning. Shaye awoke to find Victoria on deck with Noah, who'd sent Samson below for a well-earned rest.

"Well, well, if it isn't our own Florence Nightingale," Noah remarked as she approached the helm.

The last time he'd said something like that, Shaye mused, he'd called her an iron maiden. She didn't particularly care for either image, but at least she didn't hear sarcasm this time.

She had wondered how he'd greet her after the state she'd last seen him in. Some men would have been embarrassed. Others, particularly those with a macho bent—and Noah did have a touch of that—would have been defensive. But Noah seemed neither defensive nor embarrassed. He'd bounced right back to his confident self. She should have known he would.

"You're both looking chipper," she said.

Victoria smiled. "Thanks to you."

Noah seconded that. "She really is a marvel. Has an unturnable stomach and an unrivaled bedside manner."

"Mmmm. She does have a way of coaxing down medicine."

"And bathing sweaty bodies."

Victoria gaped at him. "She bathed you? I didn't get a bath!"

"I guess she can't resist a naked man."

"Naked?" She turned to Shaye, but the twinkle in her eyes took something from the horror of her expression. "Shaye, how could you?"

Before Shaye could utter a word, Noah was wailing, "There you go again—suggesting that my body's distasteful! What is it with you women?"

"I didn't suggest anything of the sort," Shaye said smoothly, and turned to Victoria. "He actually has a stunning body—a sweet little birthmark on his right hip and the cutest pair of buns you'd ever hope to see."

"I didn't think you noticed," Noah drawled to Shaye, then said to Victoria, "but don't worry. I kept the best parts hidden."

Shaye didn't answer that. She'd seen the "best parts" too, and they'd been as impressive as the rest. But she wasn't about to play the worldly woman so far that she totally cancelled out the prissy one. So she tipped back her head, to find the sky a brilliant blue. "No clouds in sight, and we're making headway again. Did we lose much ground during the storm?"

"A little," Noah answered, indulgently accepting the change in subject, "but we're back on course."

"Good." She rubbed her hands together. "Anyone want breakfast?"

Noah and Victoria exchanged a glance, then answered in unison, "Me."

"You're cooking for all of us?" Noah asked.

"I'm feeling benevolent."

He snagged her around the shoulders and drew her to his side. "Domestic instincts coming to the fore?"

"No. I'm just hungry."

"So am I."

She sent him a withering look.

He didn't wither. "Just think," he murmured for her ears alone, "how nice it would be to have breakfast together in bed."

"I never eat breakfast in bed."

"If I were still sick, would you have brought it to me there?"

"If you were still sick, you wouldn't have wanted it."

"What if my stomach was fine but my knees were so weak that I couldn't get up?"

"That'd be the day."

"You were very gentle last night. No one's taken the time to bathe me like that since I was a child."

She knew he was playing on her soft side, but before she should could come up with suitably repressive words, he spoke again.

"So you liked what you saw?"

"Oh yes. The storm was breathtaking."

"*Me*. My *body*."

"Oh, that. Well, it wasn't quite as exciting as the sea."

"Catch me tonight, and I'll show you exciting."

"Is another storm brewing?" she asked, being purposely obtuse.

Noah wasn't buying. "You bet," he said with a naughty grin.

Shaye quickly escaped from his clutches and went below to fix breakfast. Throughout the morning, though, she thought of Noah, of his body and its potential for excitement. The more she thought, the more agitated she grew.

She tried to understand what it was about him that turned her on. He was cocky and quick-tongued. He could be presumptuous and abrasive. He was, in his own way, a rebel. There were so many things not to like. Still, he turned her on.

Always before she'd been safe, and it wasn't merely a question of dating bland men. She encountered men at work, men in the supermarket, men in the bookstore, the hardware store, the laundry. She'd never given any of them a second glance.

Granted, she'd had no choice with Noah. She was stuck on a boat with him, and in such close quarters second glances were hard to avoid, particularly when the man in question made his presence felt at every turn.

Not only was she looking twice, she was also fantasizing. With vivid clarity she recalled how he'd looked naked. She hadn't been thinking lascivious thoughts at the time, but since then her imagination had worked overtime. Everything about him was manly, with a capital M—the bunching muscles of his back, the prominent veins in his forearms, the tapering of his torso, his neat, firm bottom, the sprinkling of dark hair on the backs of his thighs. And in front—she could go on and on, starting with the day's growth of beard on his face and ending with the heaviness of his sex.

If the attraction were purely physical, she could probably hold him off. But increasingly she thought of other things— his sense of humor, his intelligence, his daring, his disregard for convention—and she felt deeply threatened. Last night hadn't helped. What she'd felt when he'd been sick, when he'd needed her and she'd been there for him, came dangerously close to affection. She'd never experienced the overwhelming urge to care for a man before.

So why was it wrong? In principle, she had nothing against involvement. She supposed that some day she'd like to fall in love, just as some day she'd like to have children. She hadn't planned on falling in love now, though, when her career was in full swing. And she hadn't planned on falling in love with a man like Noah.

Not that she was in love with him, she cautioned herself quickly. But still . . .

The problem was that Noah wasn't meek. He wasn't conservative or conventional. She couldn't control him—or herself when she was with him. He was wrong for her.

Had she been in Philadelphia, she'd have run in the opposite direction. But she wasn't in Philadelphia. She was stuck on a boat in the middle of the Caribbean with Noah, and she was vulnerable. In his arms, she was lost—and she fell into his arms easily!

She'd just have to be on her guard, she decided. That was all there was to it.

THE AFTERNOON BROUGHT a torment of its own. Where the night before the wind had picked up, gusted, then positively raged, today it faded, sputtered, then died.

Shaye was sitting on deck reading when the sails began to pucker. She looked up at the mast, then at Victoria, who was sitting in blissful ignorance nearby, then down at her book again. But the sails grew increasingly limp, and at the moment of total deflation, she didn't need the unusual calm of the sea to tell her what had happened.

Noah sauntered by, nonchalantly lowering and lashing the sails.

"How long?" she asked.

He shrugged. "Maybe an hour or two. We'll see."

An hour or two didn't sound so bad. The part she didn't like was the "maybe." If their idle drifting lasted for eight hours, or sixteen, or God forbid, twenty-four...

"You look alarmed," he commented, tossing her a glance as he worked.

"No, no. I'm fine."

"View it as a traffic jam. If you were in the city, chances are you'd be on your way somewhere. But you wouldn't be able to move, so you'd be frustrated, and you'd be sick from exhaust fumes. Here you have none of that." He took a long, loud breath that expanded his chest magnificently. "Fresh air. Bright sun. Clear water. What more could you ask?"

Shaye could have asked for the wind to fill the sails and set them on their way again. The sooner they reached Costa Rica, the sooner they'd return to Colombia and the sooner she'd go home. One virile man with a magnificent chest was pushing her resolve.

"I couldn't ask for anything more," she said.

"Sing it."

"Excuse me?"

"The song. You know—" Noah jumped into a widespread stance, leaned back, extended both arms and did his best Ethel Merman imitation: "I got rhythm, I got music . . ."

She covered her face with a hand. "We did that in junior high. I believe the last line is, '*Who* could ask for anything more?'"

"Close enough."

She peered through her fingers. "Were you in the glee club?"

"Through high school. Then I was in an *a cappella* group in college. We traveled all over the place. It was really fun." His face suddenly dropped.

"What?"

"Well, it was fun for a while."

"What happened?"

He hesitated, then shrugged. "I resigned."

"Why did you do that?"

"I, uh, actually there were three of us. We got into a little trouble."

"What kind of trouble?"

He returned to his work. "It was nothing."

"What kind of trouble?"

He secured the last fold of the mainsail to the boom, then mumbled, "We went on a drinking binge in Munich. The administrators decided we weren't suitable representatives of the school."

"You didn't resign. You were kicked out."

"No, we resigned."

"It was either that or be kicked out."

He ran a hand through his hair. "You don't have to put it so bluntly."

"But that was what it boiled down to, wasn't it? You should be ashamed of yourself, Noah."

Victoria, who'd remained on the periphery of the discussion to that point, felt impelled to join in. "Aren't you being a little hard on the man, Shaye? You were in college once. You know what college kids do. They're young and having fun. They outgrow it."

"Thank you, Victoria," Noah said.

Shaye echoed his very words, but with a different inflection. She picked up her book again.

Having nothing better to do, Noah stretched out on his back in the sun. Within thirty seconds, he bobbed up to remove his shirt. Then he lay back again, folding his arms beneath his head. "I'll bet Shaye never did anything wrong in school. The model student. Hmmmm?"

Shaye didn't answer.

Victoria pressed a single finger to her lips, holding in words that were aching to spill out. Shaye shot her a warning look. The finger stayed where it was, which was both a good sign and a bad sign.

"Did you study all the time?" Noah asked.

"I studied."

"What did you do for fun?"

"Oh, this and that." She glanced toward the stern. "Where's Samson?"

"I believe he's cooking," Victoria answered, dropping her finger at last.

"What's it going to be tonight?"

Noah smirked. "Now, if he told us, it wouldn't be a surprise, and that's half the fun."

"I hate surprises."

"You hate fun. What a boring person."

"Noah," Victoria chided.

But Shaye could stand up for herself. "It's okay. I have a strong back."

"Stiff," Noah corrected in an absent tone. His eyes were closed, his body relaxed. "Stiff back. But not all the time. When I take you in my arms—"

Shaye cut him off. "Does Samson always cook foreign?"

He grinned and answered only after a meaningful pause. "Not always. He does a wicked Southern-fried chicken."

"What does he wear then?"

"I'm not telling."

She glared at him for a minute, but his eyes were still closed so he didn't see. "You wouldn't," she muttered, and returned to her book. She couldn't concentrate, of course. Not with Noah stretched out nearby. The occasional glances she darted his way brought new things to her attention—the pattern of hair swirling over his chest, the bolder tufts beneath his arms, the small indentation of his navel.

She looked back at her book, turned one page, waited several minutes, turned another. Then she set the book down in disgust. "How long have we been sitting?"

"Half an hour."

"And still no wind."

"It'll come."

"Why doesn't this boat have an engine? Nowadays every boat has an engine."

"The *Golden Echo* wasn't built 'nowadays.'"

"But she was refurbished. She has a stove and a refrigerator. Why doesn't she have an engine?"

Noah shrugged. "The Paynes must be purists."

With a snort, she picked up her book, turned several more pages, then sighed and lifted her ponytail from her neck. "Is it ever hot!"

Noah opened a lazy eye and surveyed the shorts and T-shirt she wore. "Feel free to strip."

Sending him a scowl, she pushed herself up, stalked to the companionway and went below.

He looked innocently at Victoria. "Did I say something wrong?"

Victoria didn't know whether to scold or laugh. She compromised by slanting him a chiding grin before she, too, rose.

"Hey," he called as she started off, "don't you leave me, too!"

"I'm going to visit with your uncle. It can't be much hotter down there than it is up here, and at least there's some shade."

Noah lay where he was for several minutes, then sat up and studied the horizon. He gave a voluminous sigh and pasted a jaunty smile on his face. This was what he wanted, wasn't it? Peace and quiet. The deck all to himself. He could relax if he wanted, sing if he wanted, do somersaults if he wanted.

So why did he feel restless?

Because he was hot and bothered and the damn sun wasn't helping. Abruptly dropping the smile, he surged to his feet, reached for the rope ladder, hung it from the starboard quarter, kicked off his shorts and dove into the sea. He'd done two laps around the boat when he overtook Shaye. He was as startled as she was.

"What are you doing here?" she gasped. "I thought I was alone."

"Who do you think put the ladder out?" he snapped. "And if you thought you were alone, why in the hell were you swimming? You're not supposed to swim alone."

"You were."

"That's different."

"How so?"

"I'm a man and I'm stronger."

"What a chauvinistic thing to say!"

"But it's true."

"It's absurd, and, besides, it's a moot point. You don't exactly need strength in a bathtub like this. If there were waves, there'd be a wind, and if there were a wind, we wouldn't be stuck out here floating in the middle of nowhere!"

"Always the logical answer. Y'know, Shaye, you're too rational for your own good. Ease up, will ya?"

She gave him a dirty look and started to swim around him, but he caught her arm and held it. "Let go," she ordered. "I want to swim."

"Need the exercise?"

"Yes."

"Feeling as restless as I am?"

"Yes."

"How about reckless?" he asked, his eyes growing darker.

Shaye recognized that deepening gray. His eyes went like that when he was on the verge of either mischief or passion. She didn't know which it was now, but she did know that with his hair slicked back and his lashes wet, nearly black and unfairly long, he looked positively demonic. Either that or sexy. Was she feeling reckless? "No," she stated firmly.

"Do you *ever* feel reckless?"

She shook her head.

"Not even when I take you in my arms?" He did it then, and she knew better than to try to escape. After all, he was stronger then she. "Why do I frighten you?"

"You don't."

He tipped his head to the side and gave her a reproving look.

"You don't," she repeated, but more quietly. As though to prove it—to them both—she put her hands on his shoulders.

"Are you afraid of sex?"

"I'm not a virgin."

"I know. We've been over that one before. I'm not asking whether you've done it, just whether you're afraid of it."

She was afraid of *him,* at that moment, because his mouth was so close, his lips firm and mobile. She couldn't seem to take her eyes from them. The lower was slightly fuller than its mate and distinctly sensual. Both were wet.

"Shaye?"

She wrenched her gaze to his eyes. "I'm not afraid of sex."

"Are you afraid of commitment?"

"No."

"Then why haven't you married?"

"I thought that was clear. I've been busy."

"If the right man had come along, you'd have married."

"How do you know that?"

"You ooze certain values. There's a softness to you that wouldn't be there if you were a hard-bitten career woman all the way. I have to assume that the right man just hasn't come along."

"I said that I don't date."

"You also said that you'd been involved with many men."

"But not recently. And if I don't date now, how can I possibly meet the right man?"

You don't have to date to meet men, Noah thought. *You could meet one during a vacation in the Caribbean.* "With your looks—come on, baby, with your looks the right man would make sure you dated. Him. Exclusively."

Baby. It was a stereotypically offensive endearment, yet the way he said it made her tingle. "What are you trying to prove, Noah?"

"I'm working on the theory that you turn away from men who threaten your very sane, very structured, very controlled existence. Just like you turn away from me."

"And now that you have me analyzed, you can let me go."

His arms tightened. "Hit a raw cord, did I?"

She slid her hands to his elbows and tried to push. "Not raw, nonexistent." Her teeth were gritted. "Let me go, Noah."

"I can make your body hum, but still you fight me. Why won't you let me make love to you, Shaye?"

"Because—" she was still pushing "—I don't want to."

"It'd be so easy. We could do it right here. Right now."

Her limbs were shaking, but it wasn't from the effort of trying to free herself. His tone was tender, his words electric. The combination was devastating. "Don't do this to me," she begged.

"What would I be doing that's so wrong? Is it wrong to feel drawn to someone? I do feel drawn to you, Shaye, sour moods and all."

She didn't want to hear this. Closing her eyes, she gave a firm shake of her head. "Don't say another word."

"I respect your work and your dedication to it. I respect what you feel for your aunt. I respect and admire your independence, but I want to know more about where it comes from. At the slightest mention of your family or your past, you clam up."

"I have two parents with whom I don't get along and a sister with whom I do. There. Are you satisfied?" She tried to propel herself away from him, but he wasn't letting go. She only succeeded in tangling her legs with his, which were warm, strong and very bare.

"Why don't you get along with your parents?"

"Noah, I'm getting tired. I'd like to go back on the boat."

"I'm not tired. I'll hold you. You know how."

She turned her head to the side and let out an exasperated breath. "Will you let me go?"

"No."

"I'll scream."

"Go ahead. There's no one to hear but Samson and Victoria, and they trust me." He pressed a warm kiss to her cheek, then asked gently, "Why do you do this to yourself? Why do you fight?"

His gentleness was her undoing. Suddenly tired of the whole thing, she dropped her chin to his shoulder. "Oh Lord, sometimes I wonder." Her arms slipped around him, and she felt his hands on the backs of her thighs, spreading them. In as natural a movement as she'd ever made, she wrapped her legs around his waist. "You're not wearing a suit," she murmured. "Why not?"

"I was in a rush to get in the water and there was no one around."

"Oh Noah."

He was nuzzling her ear. "What is it, hon?"

"I really am tired. I'm not used to constant sparring. I'm not good at it."

"Could've fooled me."

"All I wanted was a peaceful vacation in the Berkshires."

"Things don't always work out the way we plan. Good sometimes comes from the unexpected."

The lazy frog kick he was doing kept them bobbing gently on the sea's surface. Beneath the surface the bobbing was more erotic—the tiniest glide of their bodies against one another, a teasing, a soft simulation. Her suit was thin. She clearly felt his sex. But while her body craved the contact, she felt too spent to carry though.

"I'm so tired," she murmured, tightening her arms around him simply for the comfort of his strength.

"Things are warring inside?"

"Yes."

"Maybe if we talk it out you'll feel better."

She sighed sadly against his neck. "I don't know. For so long I've drummed certain things into my head...." Her voice trailed off.

He was stroking her back. "I'm listening."

But she couldn't go on. There were too many thoughts, too much confusion, and as comfortable as she was with him just then, she was deathly afraid of saying something she'd later regret.

"Hey," he breathed. He took her head in his hands and raised it to find her eyes brimming with tears. "Ah-h-h, Shaye," he whispered hoarsely, "don't do that. Don't torment yourself so."

She could only shut her eyes and shake her head, then cling more tightly when he hugged her again.

"I guess I've come on pretty strong."

She nodded against his neck.

"That wasn't very nice of me."

She shook her head.

"I'm really not a bad guy when you get to know me."

She was coming to see that, and it was part of the problem. Brashness she could withstand, as she could irreverence and impulsiveness. But mix any of those with gentleness, and she was in trouble.

"Come on," he said softly. His hands left her back and broke into a broad breast stroke. "Let's go back on board."

She made no effort to help him swim, and when they reached the ladder she was almost sorry to let go of him. It had been so nice holding on and being held without other threats. But she did let go and climbed the ladder, then stood on the deck pressing a towel to her face.

She heard Noah's wet feet on the wood behind her. She heard the swish of material that told her he was pulling on his shorts. For a fleeting instant she wondered whether he ever bothered with underwear, then his voice came quietly.

"Why don't you stretch out in the sun to dry? It looks like we're not going anywhere yet."

Dragging the towel slowly down her face, she nodded. Moments later, she was lying on her stomach in the sun. She cleared her mind of all but her immediate surroundings—the warmth of the sun feeling good now on her wet skin, the utter silence of the air, the gentle sway of the boat as it drifted. Noah sat nearby, but he did nothing to disturb her other than to ask if she wanted a cool drink, then fetch it when she said yes.

She knew that there were other things he could have done and said, such as stretching out beside her, offering to spread lotion on her back, suggesting that she lower the straps of her suit to avoid getting marks. He could have prodded her, pried into her thoughts, forced her to think about those things she was trying so hard to avoid.

But he did none of those things. He seemed to respect the fact that she needed a break from the battle if she was to regain her strength for the skirmishes ahead.

Late in the afternoon, Victoria joined them on deck, followed a few minutes after that by Samson. Conversation was light and for the most part flowed around Shaye. When the others decided to swim, she took her turn and savored the coolness but remained subdued, and after climbing back on board she went below to change for dinner.

When all four had gathered back on deck, Samson declared, "Nu, yesly vnyesyosh stol, Noah, ee vee pryekrasnie zhenshchina vnyes yote pagooshkee, prig at oveem yest."

"Myehdlyeenyehyeh, pahzhahloostah," Victoria requested.

Straightening the red tunic over his shorts and shirt, Samson repeated his instructions, but more slowly this time. He accompanied them with hand motions, for which Victoria was grateful. Her course in conversational Russian had only gone so far, and she was rusty.

By the time she was ready to interpret, the others had gotten the drift of Samson's request. Noah set up the table, while Shaye and Victoria brought cushions from the salon. Samson then proceeded to serve a dinner of *kulebiaka* and salad, and with a free-flowing vodka punch, the meal was lively.

Still, Shaye was more quiet than usual. She listened to the others joke about experiences they'd had, following particularly closely when Noah spoke. She learned that he'd taken Spanish through college, that he'd spent a semester in Madrid, that he'd spent the year following graduation working on a cattle ranch in Argentina. She also learned that, while there, he'd been nicknamed the Playboy of the Pampas, and though he'd been annoyed when Samson had let that little jewel slip, he hadn't denied it.

They lingered for a long time over coffee. With no wind, there was nowhere to go and no work to do. At length Samson went below deck, reappearing moments later wearing a tricorne. Then, with one of the hurricane lamps supplementing the silver light of the moon, he produced his treasure map.

Not even Shaye could resist its lure. She sat forward with the others to study the weathered piece of paper-thin parchment. "Where did you get it?" she asked.

"I was on Montserrat last winter and befriended an old British chap, who'd found it in an old desk in the villa he'd bought there fifteen years before. We'd been discussing the lore of the pirates in these parts when he brought out the map."

Victoria leaned closer to peer at the markings. "When was it supposed to have been drawn?"

"In the mid eighteen hundreds. My friend—Fitzsimmons was his name—theorized that the crew of a pirate ship stashed its booty and left, planning to return at a later, safer time."

"Only they never made it?"

"We don't know that for sure, but it's doubtful, since the map was well hidden and intact. The desk in which Fitzsimmons found it was traced back to a man named Angus Cummins, and Englishman who settled on Montserrat in the 1860s. No one seems to have known much about Cummins other than that he was a shady character, usually drunk and alone. My own research showed him to have been quartermaster on an English vessel that was shadowed by trouble. In 1859, during one of its last voyages to the Caribbean, the captain died at sea. When the boat returned to England, there were rumors of piracy and murder, but the crew stood as one and nothing was ever proven."

Victoria expelled a breath. "Murder!"

Samson shrugged. "We'll never know, but given this," he tapped the map, "there's reason to suspect that the crew was involved in piracy."

"But if that's true, why didn't Cummins—or one of the others—ever return for the treasure?" Shaye asked.

"Cummins may have been the only one with the map. As quartermaster, he was in a position of power second only to the captain. My guess is that he left England under dubious circumstances, stationed himself on Montserrat in the hope of one day crossing the Caribbean to retrieve the treasure, but never quite found the wherewithal to do it."

Assuming the accuracy of Samson's research, Noah agreed with his guess. He was skeptical, though, about the treasure still existing. "People have been searching for gold along the Costa Rican coast since Columbus dubbed the country the 'rich coast,' but the only riches discovered were bananas. If there were anything else hidden there, wouldn't it have been long since plundered?"

Feeling an odd sense of vindication, Shaye glanced at Victoria. She'd expressed a similar sentiment when Victoria had first called her about the trip.

But Samson was undaunted. "They didn't have the map." He held up a hand. "Now, I'm not saying that the treasure's there. I've checked with the Costa Rican authorities and they have no record of anyone reporting a stash being found in the area where we're headed. But that doesn't mean the treasure hasn't been stolen. Cummins may have gone back for it, then lived out his life in frustration when he realized he couldn't return to England a wealthy man. It's possible, too, that only his small portion of the take was hidden. Then again, the map may have been a fraud from the start."

Shaye leaned closer. "It looks authentic enough."

"Oh, it's authentic. At least, it was drawn during the right time period. I had it examined by experts who attested to that."

"Then how could it be fraudulent?" Victoria asked.

"Cummins may have drawn the map on a whim. He may have drawn it to indicate the spot where he'd put a treasure if he ever had one."

"You mean, there may never have been any treasure to begin with?"

"There's always that possibility." He smiled. "For the sake of adventure, though—and until we prove otherwise—we'll assume the treasure's there."

Shaye was grateful that she'd had a few drinks with dinner. Though the coffee had lessened the vodka's effects, her senses were still numbed. Had they not been, she feared she'd have said something blunt, and she didn't want to dampen Samson's enthusiasm any more than she wanted to evoke Noah's ire. "Are we talking gold?" she asked carefully.

"Most likely. Artifacts would be found in an undersea wreckage. I doubt that a man who planted a treasure with the intention of retrieving it in his lifetime would want anything but gold."

Noah was studying the map. "This spot is between Parismina and Limón?"

Samson cleared his throat, pushed the tricorne back on his head and got down to business. "That's right." His finger traced the pen scratchings. "The Costa Rican coast is lowland. Between the Nicaraguan border at the north and Puerto Limón, which lies about midway to Panama at the south, much of that lowland is swampy."

"Swampy?" Shaye cried in dismay.

"Not to worry. We're heading for a sandy spot just north of Puerto Limón, a small bay, almost a lagoon. It should be lovely."

She hoped he was right. "And once we get there . . . ?"

"Once we get there, we look for the rose."

Shaye bit her lip. She shot a glance at Victoria, then lowered her eyes to her lap.

Victoria was as dismayed as Shaye but had the advantage of being the quintessential diplomat. "An orchid I could believe," she began softly. "Orchids are the national flower. Roses, though, are not indigenous to Central America. Is it possible that a rose Cummins planted would still be alive?"

Noah chuckled as he looked from Shaye's face to Victoria's. "Tell them, Samson. They're dying."

Samson, too, was smiling. "The rose is a rock, possibly a boulder. Cummins must have taken one look at it and associated its shape with the flowers he knew from home. The treasure, if it exists, will be found in a series of paces measured from the rock."

Dual sighs of relief came from the women, causing Noah to chuckle again. But while Samson elaborated on the specifics of those paces, Shaye's thoughts lingered on the rock.

The rose. Was it pure coincidence . . . or an omen? She had a rose of her own, and it symbolized all she'd once been and done. She hid it carefully; no more than a handful of people had ever seen it. It was her personal scarlet letter, and she was far from proud of its existence.

She'd never been a superstitious person, but at that moment, she wanted nothing at all to do with the Costa Rican rose.

8

NOAH AWOKE AT EIGHT on the fourth day of the trip and lay in bed for a long time. After spending most of the night on deck, manning the sails when the wind picked up shortly after one, he'd expected to sleep later. But Shaye had invaded his dream world as much as she was invading his thoughts now that he was awake.

A change had come over her in the water yesterday, and it hadn't been a momentary thing. She'd been distracted for most of the afternoon and thoughtful for much of the evening.

Was it surrender? Not quite. She hadn't come to him that night on deck to declare her devotion and beg him to make love to her. But she did seem to have conceded to an inner turmoil. She seemed to have realized that it wouldn't just go away, that it had to be faced.

He wished he knew what was at the root of that inner turmoil, but she guarded it closely. He wasn't dumb; he knew when to push a subject and when to back off. Not that he really thought of her as a "subject." He was too personally involved for that. But his feel for people had gotten him where he was professionally, and he was counting on it now.

She'd opened up a bit before she'd gone to bed. He'd produced a deck of cards and they'd played several games of gin, and during this she'd mentioned that she and her sister, Shannon, had played gin when they'd been kids. It was one of the few things her parents had thought harmless, she'd said wryly, and when he'd teased her, she'd admitted that her parents were strict. She obviously resented that, yet from what he could see she was nearly as strict with herself as they'd been with her.

Wouldn't she have rebelled? That was what often happened to the offspring of strict parents. Or perhaps she had rebelled and been subsequently swamped by guilt. Ingrained values were hard to shake.

She was a passionate woman. He didn't doubt that for a minute. The way she'd come alive to him on those few occasions when she'd stepped out of her self-imposed mold had been telling. She had a fire inside, all right. The question was whether she'd allow it to burn.

He wasn't about to let it go out, though he was biding his time just now. He'd found her weakness and knew that when he played it soft and gentle she was more vulnerable. Yes, he was impatient; soft and gentle hadn't traditionally been strong points in his character. But then, he'd never met a woman quite like Shaye—or felt quite as compulsively drawn to one before.

He had to admit, with some surprise, that behaving softly and gently toward Shaye wasn't as much of a hardship as he might have expected. She responded well to it. Of course, that didn't mean that his loins didn't ache. He felt an utterly primal urge to make her his. But he wanted far more than a meaningless roll in the hay—or on the deck, or in a cabin, as the case might be.

Hell, where could they do it? His cabin was Samson's, too, and Shaye shared hers with Victoria. The deck was neither comfortable nor private. There was always the water, but he wanted leverage, not to mention access to certain parts of her body without fear of drowning. On the other hand, a sandy beach on the Costa Rican coast . . .

Allowing for the time they'd lost during the storm and then being becalmed, they had two days' sailing ahead before they reached their destination. Two days in which to soften her up. He'd have to work on it, he decided as he sprang from the bed and reached for a pair of shorts. He'd have to work on it, starting with a soft and gentle morning talk.

He went on deck to find Victoria and Samson but no sign of Shaye. And since he was reserving all his softness and gentleness for her, his impatience found vent in the demand, "Where is she?"

Samson tried to conceal a grin and didn't quite make it. "I haven't seen her yet this morning."

"I think she's still sleeping," Victoria added innocently. "It was after two before she finally dozed off."

A scowling Noah left them and crossed to the bow.

"Now how would you know that?" Samson drawled softly. "You were asleep yourself by eleven."

Victoria didn't ask him how *he'd* known *that*. While Noah and Shaye had been playing cards on deck, Samson had walked her to her cabin, then sat talking with her until she'd fallen asleep. She was normally a night owl, but knowing Samson relieved Noah at the helm between three and four, she'd wanted to be up soon after. Watching the sunrise with him was a memorable experience.

"Actually," she whispered, "I don't know it for sure, but I could feel her tossing and turning. And it won't do any harm to let Noah know she's losing sleep over him."

"Is that what she's doing?"

"I believe so."

He narrowed one eye. "Are you matchmaking?"

She narrowed an eye right back at him. "No more than you."

He lowered his head in that same subtle gesture of guilt that Victoria and Shaye had seen the first day. "I wasn't matchmaking, exactly," he hedged. "But when you called to say that your niece was coming along and that she was twenty-nine, attractive, intelligent and hardworking—well, I couldn't help but think of Noah."

"So you *did* get him to come after I called."

"Barney was ticked off."

"But other than what I said, you knew nothing about Shaye."

"I knew Noah. He needed a break, and not at an isolated château in Normandy. He needs a woman. He's the proverbial man who has everything... except that. Besides," he added with a roguish smile, "Garrick had told me about you, and I knew that if the niece took after the aunt in any small way..."

Victoria reached up to kiss him lightly. "You're a very sweet man. Have I told you that lately?"

"I don't mind hearing it again."

"You're a very sweet man. Thank you for the compliment... and for bringing Noah along. He and Shaye are right for each other. I just know it."

At that moment, Noah swung by en route to the companionway. "Enjoy yourselves, folks."

"Where are you off to?" Samson asked.

"Breakfast," was all Noah said before he disappeared.

It was a brainstorm, he mused as he quickly whipped up pancake batter. She was still in bed, and she hadn't eaten since dinner, and since he was hungry and she was bound to be hungry... Very innocent, he decided, it would all be very innocent. He'd simply carry in breakfast, wake her gently, and they'd eat.

As he spooned batter onto the griddle, he recalled his initial fear that she'd expect to be waited on. But he wasn't waiting on her, at least not in the sense of pandering to a woman who refused to do for herself. She'd proven more than willing to pitch in. She'd even made him breakfast yesterday.

So now he was returning the favor. Only with a sightly different twist.

A short time later, balancing the tray that Samson always used to cart food to the deck, he went to her cabin. When a light knock at the door produced no response, he quietly opened it and slipped inside. Then he stood there for a minute, stunned as always by the sight of her in bed. She was on her stomach this time, dark red hair spilling around her head, more vivid than ever against the white linens. Where the sheet left off at mid-back, her T-shirt took over in covering her completely. Still she was alluring. All white and red, primness and fire. God, was she alluring!

He quietly set the tray down by the side of the bed and perched on its edge. "Shaye?" he whispered. His hand hovered over her shoulder for a minute before lowering and squeezing lightly. "Shaye?"

She stirred, turning her head his way. Her eyes were still closed. Lock by lock, he stroked her hair back from her face.

She barely opened her mouth, and the words were slurred. "Something smells good."

"Pancakes and apple butter. I thought maybe you'd join me."

She was quiet for such a long time that he wondered if she'd fallen back to sleep. Then she murmured, "I never eat breakfast in bed."

"Are you turning down room service?"

Again a pause. Her eyes remained closed. "No."

He swallowed down a tiny sigh of relief. "Would you rather sleep a little longer?"

She yawned and struggled to open one eye. "What time is it?"

"Nine-thirty."

With a moan, she turned away. "I didn't get to bed until two."

"Get to bed" versus "doze off." Two very different connotations. "Get to bed" meant she could have been reading; he'd been on deck, so he hadn't seen whether she'd stayed in the salon for a while. "Doze off," the phrase Victoria had used, suggested that she'd tried to sleep but that her thoughts had kept her awake. He hoped it was the latter, but he wasn't about to ask. For someone who usually woke up crabby, she was in a relatively civil mood.

"Are you falling asleep on me?" he whispered.

She shook her head against the pillow.

"Just taking it slow?"

She didn't move. At length she said, "I'm trying to decide whether or not to be angry. You woke me up."

The fact that she didn't sound at all angry gave Noah hope. "I'll leave if you want. I'm hungry enough to eat both helpings."

She turned over then, pushed herself up until she was sitting against the wall, straightened the sheet across her hips and patted her lap.

With a smile he reached for the tray.

Few words were exchanged as they ate. She glanced at him from time to time, thinking how considerate it had been of him to bring her breakfast, and how good he looked even before he'd shaved, and how well he wore an unbuttoned shirt. He glanced at her from time to time, thinking how the shadows beneath her eyes had faded, and how becoming her light tan was, and how disheveled and sexy she looked.

From time to time their glances meshed, held for a second or two, broke away.

When Shaye had finished the last of her pancakes she said, "You're nearly as good a cook as Samson."

"Breakfast is my specialty."

"Between you and your uncle, you could run a restaurant."

"I have enough to do already, thank you."

She sat very still for a minute. "We're moving."

"Have been since one this morning."

She hadn't realized that and wondered how she could have been so caught up in her thoughts that she hadn't noticed.

"Want to go on deck?" Noah asked.

"I'll have to get dressed first."

"You do that while I take care of these," he said, indicating the dishes. "I'll meet you up there in, say, ten minutes?"

"Okay," she agreed quietly and watched him leave.

Ten minutes later they were standing side by side at the bow. She raised her face and closed her eyes. "Mmm, that feels good."

Noah didn't comment on the fact that she'd left her hair down, or that it was positively dancing in the breeze, or that it was tempting him nearly beyond reason. Instead he took a deep breath and asked casually, "Where do you live in Philly? An apartment?"

"Condominium. It's in a renovated building not far from the historic area."

"Is your family in Philly, too?"

"Uh-uh. Connecticut."

He turned around to lean back against the bulwark. The sails were full. He studied them, wondering if he dared ask more. Before he had a chance to decide either way, she asked, "How about you? A condo in the city?"

"Yup."

"What's your place like in Vermont?"

"Contemporary rustic."

She laughed softly. "That's honest. Most people would pride themselves on saying rustic, when in fact they have every modern amenity imaginable."

A short time later, after they'd watched a school of fish swim by, she asked, "Do you ski?"

"Sure do. You?"

"I tried a few times in college, but I never really went at it seriously."

He wanted to say that she could use his place anytime, that he'd teach her how to ski, that the most fun was après-ski, with a warm fire, a hot toddy and a bear rug before the hearth. Instead he asked what she'd been reading the day before.

Eventually they brought cushions up and made themselves more comfortable. Their talk was sporadic, never touching on deep issues, but even the trivia that emerged was enlightening.

Shaye learned that Noah was an avid Mets fan, that he want to games whenever he could spare the time, which wasn't often enough, and that he'd even became friends with a few of the players. Once he'd been mistaken for a bona fide member of the team by a small-town reporter, who interviewed him outside the locker room after a game. She learned that when he watched television, it was usually a program of the public information or documentary type. He had certain favorite restaurants he returned to often, the most notable of which was a no-name dive on the Lower East Side that had filthy floors, grumpy waiters and the best guacamole north of Chihuahua. She learned that he hated shopping, loved dressing up on Halloween—which, he assured her, came only once a year at his office—and fantasized about buying a Harley and biking across the country.

Noah learned that Shaye talked to her plants and that she generally hated to cook but could do it well when inspired. He learned that she'd always loved to read and belonged to a book group, that she wanted to take up aerobics but didn't have the time, that she liked Foreigner, Survivor, and Chicago but never went to live rock concerts.

The day passed with surprising speed. Shaye wasn't quite sure whether the new Noah, the one who was companionable rather than seductive, was the real Noah. But since he'd offered her a respite from the torment he'd previously inflected, she wasn't about to raise the issue aloud.

Her subconscious wasn't quite as obedient. No sooner had she gone to bed that night than the sensual Noah popped up in her dreams, only it was worse, now, because the man who excited her physically was the same one she'd begun to respect. She awoke in a frenzy, torn apart and sweaty, and immediately put the blame on the Vietnamese dinner Samson had prepared that night. By the next morning, though, that excuse had worn thin. One look at Noah, freshly shaved and wearing nothing but a low-slung pair of shorts, stirred her blood.

She fought it all day, but to no avail. They were together nearly constantly, and though he didn't fall back on either double entendres or provocative observations, his eyes held the dark sexuality that expressed her own deepest thoughts. She was acutely, viscerally, passionately aware of him.

While they ate breakfast, which he consumed in bulk and with enthusiasm, she was entranced by his mouth. It was mobile and firm, yet sensual. She couldn't help but recall how aggressively it had consumed her own, and when her eyes met his for a fleeting moment, she knew he was remembering the same.

Later she sat with him on deck while he cleaned the hurricane lamps, his long, lean fingers working the cloth over brass. She was mesmerized by those fingers and finally had to tear her eyes away, but the memory of them working her breasts with agile intimacy caused a rush of warmth to spread beneath her skin. Noah didn't comment on the blush or on the sudden shift of her gaze, but when she dared look back at him, she caught a starkly hungry expression.

Later still, when he relieved Samson at the helm, she relaxed against the transom—or she'd intended to relax, until Noah's bold stance commanded her attention. He had a beautiful body and he held it well, shoulders back, head up. Whether standing with his legs spread or with his ankles crossed or with his weight on one hip, he oozed self-confidence. And when he walked, as he did to occasionally adjust the sails, he oozed masculinity. She wondered what it was about tight-hipped men who moved with nothing more than the subtlest shift of their bottoms—whether it was the economy of movement that made a woman greedy, or the pelvic understatement that was overwhelmingly suggestive, or simply the fact that between waist and thigh men were built so differently from women.

Of course, she couldn't remember ever having taken much notice of men's bottoms before, not even in the old days. So it had to be Noah.

Self-confident, sexy, every move natural and spontaneous. He wasn't a preener. Not one of his motions seemed tutored. His body was simply...his body. And his very indifference to it made him all the more attractive to Shaye.

And all *that* was before she got down to the details. The roughened skin on his elbows...the compact lobes of his ears...the symmetry of his upper back, the gleam of sunbronzed skin over flexing muscles...the shallow dip at his hipline just before his shorts cut off the view... So many things she wanted to touch, so many things that touched her even without actual physical contact.

Like his chest. Noah's chest inspired wanton behavior. She wanted to feel its varying textures, to touch her finger to a smooth spot, a hairy spot, a firm spot, a soft spot. His nipples were small in that male kind of way, but that didn't mean there was anything less intimate about them. The more she looked, the more intimately she was moved.

In the end, though, it was his eyes, always his eyes that touched her most deeply. To say that his eyes stripped her naked was too physical a description. They delved far deeper, burrowing beneath her skin and touching hidden quarters that no man, *no* man had ever touched. With each look she felt his thoughts, and she knew that he wanted her.

So the sexual tension built. What had rippled in the morning was simmering by noon and smoldering three hours later. The air between them grew positively charged, but they could no more have left each other's sides than they could have denied that the charge existed.

Then, shortly before five, a low shadow materialized on the distant horizon.

"Land, ho!" Noah shouted from the bow, grateful to relieve his tension with the hearty yell.

Shaye was at his elbow. "Costa Rica?"

"It had better be," he said, "or we're in trouble."

She knew he wasn't referring to an accidental landing in another country. They needed a diversion, and they needed one fast.

"What happens now?" Victoria asked, joining them.

Noah and Shaye exchanged a quick, hot look. "Now," he said, "we try to find out exactly where we are."

Samson was already doing that, working with binoculars, a compass, and the charts and notes he'd made. "We're pretty much on target," he finally announced to his waiting audience. "Assuming that the cargo ships we've seen are heading for either Limón or Moín, all we need to do is to sail a little north. Once we're in closer, I'll know more."

It took a while, for the wind lessened the closer they got, but they gradually worked their way in the right direction. Shaye, who'd begun the trip with a minimum of enthusiasm for Costa Rica, couldn't deny the country's tropical beauty. Spectral mountains provided a distant backdrop for the lush jungle growth that grew more delineated as they neared the shore. The graceful fronds of tall palms arched over small stretches of sandy beach. Thicker mangroves and vines populated swampier sections.

They approached a small bay, and three pairs of eyes sought Samson's. But he shook his head. "The configuration is wrong."

"Perhaps it's changed with time?" Shaye asked.

"Not that much," was his answer. So they sailed on.

After a time they neared another sandy area. Low outcroppings of rock lay at either end, curving out to give a lagoon effect. "Could be," Samson said. "It's broad enough in the middle, flat enough from front to back.... Could be," he repeated, this time with enthusiasm. "I won't know for sure until can take a reading with the sextant, and it looks like the stars will be elusive for a while."

Those three pairs of eyes joined him in scanning the cloud cover that was fast moving in.

Recalling how sick she'd been on the second night of the trip, Victoria asked with a touch of horror, "Another storm?"

"Probably nothing more than rain," Noah guessed, then asked Samson, "Should we go in and drop anchor?"

"That's our best bet."

By the time the *Golden Echo* was anchored about two hundred yards from shore, night had fallen. The four gathered in the salon, with an air of great expectancy.

"This is frustrating," Victoria decided. "To be here and not really know whether we are, in fact, here...."

"Patience," Samson urged with a smile. "We'll know soon enough. We've made good time, and I've allowed five days to search for the treasure. That's far more than we should need once we reach the right lagoon. Even if this one isn't it, we can't be far."

Shaye's eyes met Noah's for a minute before slanting away.

Victoria's eyes were on Samson. "How does the Costa Rican government take to treasure hunts like ours?"

"I filed the proper papers and was granted a permit. The government has a right to half of anything we recover."

Victoria knew by this time that Samson had as little need of gold as she did. "What will you do with it?"

"The treasure? Of the half that's left, only a quarter will be mine." His gaze skipped meaningfully from one face to another.

"I don't want any treasure," Shaye said quickly. It had never occurred to her that she'd receive a thing, and picturing the rose-shaped rock, she felt vehement about it.

"Count me out, too," Noah said forcefully. He looked at Shaye, and his eyes grew smoky. *There are many different kinds of treasure. . . .*

"I'm bequeathing my portion to you," Victoria informed Samson. "Lord only knows I pay enough in taxes now." She settled more comfortably onto the sofa. "What will you do with it?"

Samson gave a quick shrug. "Give it to charity—four times as much as I'd originally planned."

Victoria grinned. "I like that idea. What do you think, Shaye?"

Shaye's head popped up. She'd been studying her knotted hands, wishing that they could somehow take the tension from inside her and wring it away. "Excuse me?"

"Charity. Samson plans to give our treasure to charity."

"I like that idea."

Victoria laughed. "That was what I said."

"Oh."

"How about you, Noah?" Samson asked. "Any objections?"

Hearing his name, Noah tore his gaze from Shaye. "To you and Victoria splitting the treasure?"

Samson sighed. "To my giving the entire thing to charity."

"I like that idea," Noah said, then frowned when both Samson and Victoria laughed. He'd obviously missed something, but he didn't know what it was. He did know that he was the brunt of the joke. Then again, Shaye wasn't laughing.

Victoria took pity on him and turned to Samson with what she hoped was a suitably serious expression. "What's for dinner tonight?"

"Bologna sandwiches."

"Bologna sandwiches?"

"That's right."

Neither Noah nor Shaye showed the slightest reaction to his announcement. They were alternately looking at each other, looking at the floor, looking at Samson or Victoria for the sake of politeness. They saw little, heard even less.

"So you finally got tired of cooking," Victoria declared with relief. "You're human, after all."

Arching a brow her way, Samson grabbed her hand, pulled her from the sofa and made a beeline for the galley, muttering under his breath, "I could probably open a can of dog food and neither of them would notice."

He was right. Neither Noah nor Shaye commented on the artlessness of the menu, though both drank their share of the Chianti Samson decanted.

Shaye tried, really she did, to concentrate on the dinner conversation, but her thoughts and senses were too filled with Noah to allow space for much else.

Noah tried every bit as hard to interject a word here or there to suggest he was paying attention, but more often than not the word was inappropriate, several sentences too late or offered in a totally wrong inflection.

They roused a bit when it began to rain and everything had to be carried below deck in a rush, but the alternate arrangements had them sitting close together in the galley. Not only was sane thought all the harder, but the tension between them rose to a fevered pitch.

"Why don't we adjourn to the salon and finish the wine?" Samson suggested at last. "There's no reason why Chianti won't go with Ding-Dongs."

"You didn't bring Ding-Dongs," Victoria chided.

"I certainly did. Next to chocolate mousse, Ding-Dongs are my favorite dessert."

Neither Noah nor Shaye had a word to say about Ding-Dongs, but they came to when Samson and Victoria rose to leave. "I'll clean up," they offered in unison, then eyed each other.

Shaye said, "You go on into the salon with the others. I'll take care of this."

Noah said, "There isn't much. I don't mind. You go relax."

"I've been relaxing all day. I'd like to do something."

"And I feel guilty because my uncle has been the major cook. The least I can do is clean up."

"Noah, I'll do it." She started stacking dirty plates.

He had the four wineglasses gathered, a finger in each. "*I'll* do it."

"We wanted those glasses," Samson remarked.

Noah sent him a confused look. "I thought we were done."

"I had suggested that we finish the wine in the salon."

"Oh." He looked down at the glasses. "But they're mixed up now. I don't know whose is whose."

"Obviously," said Samson, whereupon Noah turned on Shaye.

"If you hadn't been so stubborn, this wouldn't have happened."

"Me, stubborn? You were the one who was being difficult."

"How can you say that someone offering to do the dirty work is being difficult?"

"*I* offered to do the dirty work *first*."

"Then *you* were the one who was difficult, when all I wanted was to relieve you of the chore."

"But I didn't *want* to be relieved—"

Victoria cut her off with a loud declaration. "We'll take clean glasses." She did just that and led Samson from the galley.

Shaye attacked the dishes with a vengeance.

"Take it easy on the water," Noah snapped. "There's no need to run more than you need."

"I need *some*, if you want the plates clean."

"Of course I want the plates clean, but you could be economical."

She thrust a dripping plate his way. "Dry this."

"You're very good at giving orders. Is that what you do all day at work?"

"At least I don't get any back talk there."

"I'm sure they wouldn't dare or you'd boot them out. I assume," he drawled, "that you have the power to hire or fire."

"In my department, I certainly do. Lawyers know nothing about computers or the people who use them."

He held up the plate he'd been drying and asked with cloying sweetness, "Is this shiny enough for Her Highness?"

She simply glared at him and handed him another, then started on the next with a double dose of elbow grease.

"You're gonna break that plate if you're not careful."

She ignored him. "And you're a fine one to talk. You're the head of your own company—a power trip if there ever was one. I'll bet *you* run a tight ship. A regular Captain Bligh."

"I have high standards, as well I should. My name's on top. I get the blame when someone flubs up."

"And the same isn't true for me? Don't you think the lawyers get on *my* back when documents come out screwed up?"

"What I want to know," he snarled, "is if they ever get you *on* your back."

The glass she'd been scrubbing came close to breaking against the sink. "You have the filthiest mind I've ever been exposed to!"

"And who's been fueling it? Little looks here, darting glances there. I'm not made of stone, for Christ's sake!"

She'd rinsed off the glass she'd nearly broken and was onto another. "Could've fooled me. Your eyes are as lecherous as your mind. You sit there making me squirm, and what do you expect me to do—whistle 'Dixie'?"

"You couldn't whistle if you tried. Your lips are too stiff."

"It's a lucky thing they are. Anything but a stiff lip around you would result in a physical attack."

"I have never physically attacked a woman in my life! But I'm beginning to wonder about you and that past you try so hard to hide. It comes out, y'know. I can see it in your eyes. You've had sex, and you've had it but good. What was it— with a married guy? Or a highly visible guy you're determined to protect?"

"You're out in left field, Noah." She thrust a handful of forks and knives at him, then, having run out of things to wash, went at the sink itself.

"I think it was with a married guy. You fell in love, gave him everything and only after the fact learned that he wasn't yours for the taking."

"Dream on." She began to wipe down the table with a fury.

"Either that, or you're totally repressed. Your parents instilled the fear of God in you and you're afraid to do a damn thing. But the urges are there. You live them vicariously through sexy rock ballads, but you don't have the guts to recognize what you need."

"And you know what that is, I suppose?"

"Damn right I do. You need a man and lots of good, old-fashioned loving. You may like to think of yourself as a prim and proper old maid, but I've seen your true colors. They're hot and vibrant and dripping with passion."

She turned to him, hands on her hips, nostrils flaring. "What I need is none of your business. I sure don't need *you*."

"You need a man who's forceful. I fight you, and I'd wager that's a hell of a lot more than any other man has ever done."

"Power trip, ego trip—they're one and the same with you, aren't they?" Throwing the damp rag into the sink, she whirled around and stalked out of the galley. A second later she was back, glowering at Noah while she reached for a clean wineglass.

Snatching up his own, he followed her. He filled it as soon as she'd set down the bottle, then took his place in the same chair he'd had before dinner.

"We were talking about pirates," Victoria said. She and Samson sat on the sofa, hard-pressed to ignore the foul moods the newcomers were in. "Samson's done a lot of reading. He says that many of the stereotypes are wrong."

"In what way?" Shaye demanded.

Noah grunted. "They were frustrated men, stuck on a boat without a willing woman to ease their aches."

"Not every man is fixated on his libido," she snapped, then turned to Samson. "Tell me about pirates."

"Pirates turn you on, huh?"

"Keep quiet, Noah. You were saying, Samson..."

"I was saying that when one begins to study the age of piracy, one learns some interesting things. For example, pirates rarely flew the skull and crossbones. They rarely made anyone walk the plank. They rarely marooned a man."

Noah snorted. "And when they did, they left him a pistol so that he could put an end to his misery. That's compassion for you."

"I'm not trying to idealize the buccaneer, simply to point out that he was more than a blood-thirsty ruffian with no respect for life. Pirates had their own kind of code."

"Nonpolitical anarchy," was Noah's wry retort.

"It worked for them," Samson said. "They chose their captains at will and could dismiss them as easily."

"Dismiss or execute?"

"Noah, let the man talk."

Noah slid lower in his chair. His brows formed a dark shelf over his eyes, but he said nothing.

"They did execute their captains on occasion," Samson conceded, "but only when those captains mistreated them. You have to understand that most of the men who crewed on pirate ships had known the brunt of poverty, or religious or political persecution at home. Fair treatment was one of the few benefits of piracy."

"But what about the gold they captured?" Shaye asked. "Didn't they benefit from that?"

Noah looked her in the eye. "They blew it on women in the first port they hit. I hope to hell the doxies were worth it."

"You'll never know, will you?" she asked sweetly.

He glared at her. She glared right back. Then he bolted from his chair and stormed toward the companionway.

"Where are you going?"

"Out."

"But it's raining!"

"Good!"

Shaye dragged her gaze back to the salon. She looked first at Victoria, then at Samson. "He's impossible!"

Samson contemplated that for a minute, then went on in his customary gentle voice, "The popular image is that pirates were irreligious plunderers who had a wonderful time for themselves, but it wasn't so. They were unhappy men. With each voyage, their hopes of returning home dimmed. It didn't matter that home wasn't wonderful. Home was familiar. It had to have been frustrating."

Shaye dropped her gaze to her hands. Victoria took up the slack and continued talking with Samson, but it wasn't until Noah reappeared that Shaye raised her eyes.

He was soaking wet and impatient. "Come on," he said, grabbing her hand.

"What—"

"We'll be back," he called over his shoulder as he led her toward the companionway.

"Hold on a minute." She tugged back on her hand. "I'm not going up there."

But he refused to let go, and he wasn't stopping. "You won't melt." He pushed the hatch open and had pulled her through before she could do anything about it.

9

THE RAIN was a warm, steady shower, drenching Shaye within seconds. "Noah, this is crazy!"

He loomed over her, the outline of his face glistening in the light of the lamp that hung at the stern. "We're going ashore."

"But it's pouring!"

Plowing his fingers into her hair, he took her mouth in a kiss that was as fevered as the tension had been earlier, as hungry as he'd felt all day, as wild as he'd ever been at his boldest moments. By the time he raised his head, Shaye was reeling.

"We're going ashore," he repeated hoarsely.

The night was dark and stormy, but that meager light from the stern clearly illuminated the intent on his face and the desire in his eyes. At that moment, she knew precisely what he had in mind. And she knew at that moment that she wouldn't refuse him. The flame within her was too hot to be denied. It blotted out everything but a basic, driving need.

"How?" she whispered shakily.

"The dingy." Snatching up a huge flashlight, he aimed it over the side of the boat, where the small rubber lifeboat he'd just inflated bobbed in the rain. Then he swung onto the rope ladder and started down. Midway, he waited for Shaye. When she was just above him, he lowered himself into the raft. As soon as she was safely settled, he began to row quickly toward shore.

With a trembling hand, Shaye tossed back her dripping hair. She didn't know whether what she was doing was right, but she knew that she had no choice. The darkness abetted her primal need; it erased reality, leaving only the urgency of the moment. Her entire body shook in anticipation of the intimacy she was about to share with Noah. Her eyes were locked on his large dark form throughout the brief trip, receiving an unbroken message that sizzled through the rainy night.

The dingy touched shore with a quivering bump. Noah jumped out seconds before Shaye, made a brief survey of the beach with the light, then dropped it and, in a single flowing movement, whipped the boat onto the sand and reached for her.

She was made for his arms, fitting them perfectly. Her hands went into his wet hair as her open mouth met his. Tension, hunger, fierceness—the combined effect was galvanic. His tongue plunged deeply. She nipped it, sucked it, played it wildly with her own.

With a groan, Noah set frenzied fingers to work tugging the soaked T-shirt from her body. But he was unwilling to release her mouth for an instant, so he abandoned it at her shoulders and dug his fingers under the waistband of her shorts. She helped him in the tugging, her lips passionate beneath his all the while. As soon as the soggy cotton passed her knees, she kicked free of the shorts and turned her efforts to Noah's. They'd barely hit the sand when he dropped his hands to her thighs and lifted her onto his waiting heat.

At the bold impaling, Shaye cried out.

"It's okay, baby," he soothed, panting. "It's okay."

She gasped his name and clung to his neck. "I feel so full..."

"You're hot and tight around me. Ahh, you feel good!" His fingers dug into her bottom, holding her bonded to him as he sank to his knees. "Have I hurt you?" he asked between nips at her mouth.

"No. Oh, no."

"I was afraid you'd change your mind, and I couldn't last another minute without being inside." His hands had risen to cover her breasts, stroking her through silk, then hastily releasing the front catch of her bra and seeking out her naked flesh.

Again she cried out. His fingers were everywhere, circling her, kneading her, daubing her nipples with raindrops. She was in a lagoon. She couldn't see the lagoon or the jungle, but she knew it was paradise, she just knew it, and with less thought than Eve she gave in to temptation.

Her hands began a greedy exploration under his shirt, over his waist, across his buttocks, up and down his thighs. He wasn't moving inside her, but she could feel every inch of him against her moist sheath, and the solid stimulation was breathtaking. Whispering his name, she tried to move her hips. But he followed the movement with his own, preventing even the slightest withdrawal.

"You're mine now," he said with the tightness of self-restraint. "We'll take it slow."

She raked her teeth against his jaw. "I want to feel you move."

"Soon, baby. Soon."

His mouth plundered hers. His thumbs began a slow, sliding rotation of her nipples. Live currents snapped and sizzled so hotly inside her that she almost feared she'd be electrocuted in the rain. Noah was grounding her, she told herself, yet still she burned. She caught at his hair and kissed him more deeply. She drew her nails across his shoulders, then dug them in and tried to move again, but he wouldn't have it.

"Noah . . ."

He worked her T-shirt over her head and pushed the bra straps from her shoulders, leaving her naked in the night but hot, so hot against him. "Soon," he murmured thickly.

"Soon." The last was breathed against her breast moments before he sucked her in.

For a minute all she could do was hold his head. Her own was thrown back, her eyes were closed, and the rain was as gentle, as persistent and seductive as his ever-moving tongue. With the visual deprivation imposed by the night, her senses grew that much sharper. She felt everything he did with vivid clarity, and the knot of need inside her grew tighter.

Shaye wondered where he got his self-control and vowed to break it. While her mouth grew more seductive, her hands taunted his chest. Short, wet hairs slid between her marauding fingers and his nipples grew hard. She undulated her middle, then, when he clutched her there to hold her still, her hips. She felt him quiver insider her, and, encouraged, repeated the motion.

But through it all there was something more. Instead of simply snapping his control, she wanted to give him a pleasure so hot and intense that he'd be branded every bit as deeply as she was. Bent on that, she reached low and stroked that part of him that hung so heavily between his thighs.

The bold caress was his undoing. Making a low, guttural sound, he tumbled her down to the sand. Bowing his back, he withdrew, then thrust upward with a force that thrilled her. She'd been right to want movement, for the friction, the sliding pressure was exquisite. But Noah had been right, too, for the wait had enhanced both her desire and appreciation.

He set a masterful rhythm that varied with their needs. Faster or slower, she met him and matched him, each arching stroke stretching the heavenly torment into an ever-tautening fine wire.

The tension snapped with a final, agonizingly deep thrust. Implosion and explosion, simultaneous and mind shattering, sent blind cries slicing through the beat of the rain. Soft gasps followed, an occasional whimper from Shaye, a moan from Noah. They clung tightly to each other until they were totally limp, and then the rain began to soothe their bodies, cleansing, cooling and replenishing.

When Noah had regained a modicum of strength, he maneuvered them both into the kneeling position from which they'd fallen. He wasn't ready to leave Shaye, and given the renewed strength of her hold, he suspected he'd have been unable to if he tried. It was gratifying, the perfect denouement to what had been a heartrending experience.

He spread his hands over her bare back, able to savor now the delight of her shape as he hadn't had the patience to do earlier. "I knew it would be like that," he murmured. "We're like tinder, Shaye. All it takes is a single match and we go up." He gave a throaty laugh. "I'm still up."

She could feel that. Oh, she could feel it, and she was astonished to find that corresponding parts of her were similarly alert. "You're a powerful lover," she whispered. It was an understatement, but she didn't think the words existed to adequately describe what she'd felt.

"I could say the same about you," he whispered back. He was thinking that he didn't care how many other lovers she'd had or who had first awakened her to the fiery art of passion, but he didn't say so. It wasn't that he didn't want to know, because that jealous male part of him did, but he didn't want to disturb the precious peace that existed between them. So he asked, "Do you mind the rain?"

"No. There's something erotic about it."

"There's something erotic about this whole setting. I wish to hell I could see it."

Resting her cheek on his shoulder, she chuckled. She knew what he meant. But then, she needed the darkness. She didn't want to see herself, and she didn't want Noah to see her. There was still the matter of the small mark on her breast; she had no idea how she would explain it, whether she wanted to, what the ramifications would be. Too much thought at too sensitive at time...she was still into feeling, rather than thinking.

"Take off your shirt," she whispered, then slid her hands to his waist to hold their bodies together while he complied. When he was as naked as she, she wrapped her arms around his neck, bringing her breasts into contact with his chest for the very first time.

The feeling was heavenly. She moved gently against him. He sucked in a shaky breath, and when she felt him swell inside her, her muscles automatically tightened.

"Ohh, baby..."

"You can feel that?" She smiled when his groan clearly indicated that he could, but then he was kissing her smile away and touching her in ways that reduced her to quivering jelly. She sighed when he released her mouth, only to gasp when he slid a hand between their bodies and began an ultra-sensitive stroking. It wasn't long before she reached a second fierce climax.

She was panting against his shoulder, her hands grasping his chest, thumbs on his nipples, when he went tense, uttered a strangled cry and pushed more deeply into her. She felt the spasms that shook him, felt his warmth flowing into her and knew an incredible joy.

"Ahh, Shaye," he whispered when he could finally speak, "you're amazing."

She basked in the glow of his words. She'd heard similar ones before, but never spoken with quite the same awe, and that meant the world to her. Pressing her face to his neck, she nestled into his arms. It was apparently the right thing to do, for he held her closely and seemed as satisfied as she with the silence.

At length, though, it occurred to her that a rainy Eden had its drawbacks. She wanted a bed. She wanted to lie down beside Noah in the darkness, to breathe in his undiluted scent, to hear the unaccompanied beat of his heart. She wanted to rest in his arms, just rest. She was suddenly very tired.

"I think we'd better go back," he murmured into her hair.

She wondered if he'd read her mind. His voice sounded as tired as she felt. More than that, it contained a note of sadness that she understood; no matter how they looked at it, there wasn't a bed for them to share.

She let him help her to her feet and together they retrieved their clothing. As though afraid of breaking the spell further, Noah didn't turn on the flashlight. He set the dingy in the water, helped Shaye inside, then climbed in and more slowly rowed back to the *Golden Echo*. As had been the case during the trip to shore, her eyes held him the entire way back. This time, though, rather than the heat of desire, she felt something even deeper and more tender. Shaye wasn't about to put a name to it any more than she was ready to face what it entailed. She simply wanted it to go on and on.

After securing the dingy to the stern of the sloop, they climbed back on deck. Holding Shaye's hand firmly in his, Noah cast a despairing glance at the rain that continued to pour. Then he guided her down the companionway and closed the hatch.

"Want to change into dry things and sit in the salon for a little while?" he asked softly.

She nodded, but still she didn't move. Their fingers were interlaced; she tightened hers. She feared that even the briefest parting would allow for an unwelcome intrusion.

Noah raised her hand and gently kissed each of her fingers, then lowered his head and gently kissed her mouth. "Go," he whispered against her lips. "I'll be waiting for you."

Determined to change as quickly as possible, she whirled around and promptly stumbled. She'd have fallen to the floor had not Noah caught her. While he held her to his side, he frowned at the cause of her near-accident. A large bundle and one about half its size were stacked in the passageway by the aft cabin.

"My duffel bags?" he asked softly. His confused gaze shifted to Shaye before returning to the bundles. "Packed?" He stared at them a minute longer, then, with dawning awareness, broke into a lopsided grin. "I'll be damned...."

Shaye left his side long enough to check out the forward cabin. It was empty. "They must both be in your cabin," she whispered, draping an arm around his neck in delight.

"Looks that way."

"But... how did they know?"

"Maybe they had the dingy bugged."

"Impossible."

"Then they're simply very wise people."

"Or very selfish."

"Hell, they deserve pleasure, too. On the other hand, maybe they meant this as punishment for the way I behaved earlier."

"You could be right."

He scowled. "That's not what you were supposed to say."

Her eyes turned innocent, while her heart positively brimmed. "What was I supposed to say?"

"That I was only being ornery out of frustration." His whisper grew softer. "Are you going to make me sleep on the couch?"

She gave a quick shake of her head.

"I can share your bed?"

She nodded as quickly.

"Because you feel sorry for me?"

"Because I want you with me."

His smile was so warm then, so filled with satisfaction that she knew a hundred-fold return on her honesty. He didn't make a smug comment on her primness, or lack thereof. He didn't accuse her of being wanton. He just smiled, and another bit of the retaining wall surrounding her defenses fell away.

Without a word, he scooped up his bags and followed her to the forward cabin. Once side, he dropped his things and took her in his arms. He didn't kiss her. He didn't caress her. He simply held her.

"Shall I light the lamp?" he asked quietly.

"No."

"I'd like to get out of these wet things."

"Me, too."

"Got a towel?"

She nodded, and when he released her, went to get it. He'd shed his shorts and shirt by the time she returned with the towel, and by the time she'd wrestled her way out of her own things, he was ready to dry her. There was nothing seductive in his touch; it was infinitely gentle and made her feel more special than she'd ever felt before. The feeling remained when they curled next to each other in bed, and it was so strong and gave her such confidence that she probably would have answered any question he'd asked just then.

He only asked one thing. "Comfortable?"

"Mmm."

He was quiet for a time before he spoke. "There is such pleasure in this. Just lying here. Close."

"I know," she whispered and softly kissed his chest.

"I just want to hold you."

"Me, too."

"I want you with me when I wake up."

"I will be."

"You can kick me if I snore."

She yawned. "Okay."

"If Samson wakes us at five to go digging for his damned treasure, I'll wring his neck."

"I'll help you."

"On the other hand," he added, his voice beginning to slur, "maybe they'll sleep late themselves."

"Or maybe they'll take pity on us."

"Fat chance . . ."

"Mmm . . ."

ALL THINGS WERE relative. The knock on the door didn't come until eight the next morning, but Shaye and Noah weren't ready for it even then. They'd been awake on and off during the night and were dragged out of a sound sleep by Samson's subsequent shout.

"We've been waiting for two hours! Can you give us an ETA?"

"That's Expected Time of Arising," Victoria called.

After bolting upright in alarm, Noah collapsed, burying his face in Shaye's hair. "Make them go away," he whispered.

"Noon!" she shouted to the two beyond the door.

"Noon?" Victoria echoed. "That's obscene!"

Samson agreed. "If you think we're going to wait until noon to go ashore, think again!"

"Go ashore," Shaye suggested, tugging the sheet higher. "I'll just sleep a little longer."

"But I need Noah's help," Samson argued.

"He's on shore. I left him there last night."

"What do you mean, you left him there?"

"He was behaving like a jackass." She twisted over Noah to muffle his snicker. "What choice did I have? And it's a good thing I did leave him there. Exactly where did you expect him to sleep?"

There was silence on the other side of the door, so she went on. "That was a fine stunt you two pulled—behaving like a pair of oversexed teenagers." Noah nuzzled her collarbone.

She slid to her side again and wrapped her arms around his neck. "What kind of an example is that to set? I have to say that I was a little shocked—"

Her words were cut off by the abrupt opening of the door. Victoria stood with one hand on the knob, the other on her hip. Samson was close behind her. Their eyes went from Shaye to the outline of bodies beneath the sheet.

"I am assuming," Victoria said drolly, "that Noah is hidden somewhere under that mane of hair. Either that, or you've grown an extra body, a pair of very long legs and a dark beard."

"Tell her to go away," came Noah's muffled voice.

"Go away," Shaye said.

"ETA?" Samson prodded.

"Noon."

Victoria made a face. "Nine."

"Eleven."

"Ten," said Samson. "Ten, and not a minute later." He raised his voice. "Do you hear me, Noah?"

Noah groaned. "I hear."

"Good. Ten o'clock. Topside." His hand covered Victoria's as he pulled the door shut.

Closing her eyes, Shaye slid lower to lay her head on Noah's chest. He wrapped an arm around her back and murmured, "I'd like to stay here all day."

"Mmm."

"Sleep well?"

"Mmm."

"Shaye?" He began to toy with her hair.

"Mmm?"

"That little mark on your breast. What is it?"

Her eyes came open and for several seconds she barely breathed. "Nothing," she said at last.

"It isn't nothing. It looks like a tattoo."

She was silent.

"Let me see."

She held him tighter.

"Shaye, let me see." Taking her shoulders, he set her to the side. His eyes didn't immediately lower, though, but held hers. "You didn't really hope to hide it forever, did you?" he asked gently. "I've touched and tasted every part of you. There's pleasure to be had from looking, too."

She bit her lip, but she knew that she wouldn't deny him. If he'd sounded smug or lecherous, she'd have been able to put up a fight. But against gentleness she was helpless.

Very carefully he eased the sheet away. He sat up and pushed it lower, then leaned back on his elbow while his eyes began at her toes and worked their way upward. His hand followed, skimming her calves and her thighs, brushing lightly over auburn curls before tracing her hip bones and belly to her waist.

His hand was growing less steady. He swallowed once and took a deep breath. "Your body is lovely," he whispered as his eyes crept higher. He touched her ribs, then slowly, slowly outlined her breasts.

She'd been lying on her left side. Gently rolling her to her back, he brought a single forefinger to touch the small mark that lay just above her pounding heart.

"A rose," he breathed. It was less than half the size of his smallest fingernail, delicately etched in black and red. His gaze was riveted to it. "When did you get it?"

"A lifetime ago," she whispered brokenly.

"Why?"

"It . . . I . . . on a whim. A stupid whim."

"You don't like it?"

She shook her head, close to tears. "But I can't make it go away."

Lowering his head, he kissed it lightly, then dabbed it with the tip of his tongue. "It's you," he whispered.

"No!"

"Yes. Something hidden. A secret side."

She was clenching her fists. "Please cover it up," she begged.

He did, but with his mouth rather than with the sheet, and at the same time he covered the rest of her body with his. "You are beautiful, tattoo and all. You make me burn." Holding the brunt of his weight on his forearms, he moved sensuously over her.

Shaye, too, burned. She'd lost track of the number of times they'd made love during the night, but still she wanted him. There was something about the way she felt when he made love to her—a sense of richness and completion. When he possessed her, she felt whole. When she was with him, she felt alive.

It didn't make sense that she should feel that way, when what she'd found with Noah was a moment out of time, when he was everything she'd sworn she didn't want, when he was everything she feared. But it wasn't the time to try to make sense of things. Not with his lips closing over hers and his hand caressing her breast. Not with their legs tangling and their stomachs rubbing. Not with his sex growing larger by the minute against her thigh.

Raising her knees to better cradle him, she responded ardently to his kisses. She loved the firmness of his lips and their mobility, just as she loved the feel of his skin beneath her fingers. His back was a broad mass of ropy muscles, his hips more narrow and smooth. The heat his body exuded generated an answering heat. His natural male scent was enhanced by that of passion.

Slowly and carefully, he entered her. When their bodies were fully joined, his back arched, his weight on his palms, he looked down at her and searched her eyes. "I want to see this, too," he said hoarsely. His breathing was unsteady. The muscles of his arms trembled. He was working so hard to rein in the same desires that buzzed through her, and he was doing so much better a job of it than she, that she broke into a sheepish smile.

Carefully he brought her up onto his lap, then, hugging her to him, inched his way backward until he'd reached the edge of the bed. When he slid off to kneel on the floor, she tightened the twist of her ankles at the small of his back. Not once was the penetration broken.

Shaye couldn't believe what happened then. Where another man would have simply begun to move while he watched, Noah cupped her face and kissed her deeply. He worshipped her mouth, her cheeks, her chin. He plumped up her breasts with his hands and devoured them as adoringly. And only when she was thinking she'd die from the searing bliss did he lower his gaze. Hers followed.

He withdrew and slowly reentered. A long, low moan slipped from his throat. His head fell back, eyes momentarily closed against the enormity of sensation.

Needing grounding of her own, Shaye looped her arms around his neck and dropped her forehead to his shoulder. She was panting softly. Her insides were on fire. She was stunned by the depth of emotion she felt, the profoundness of what they were doing, the overwhelming sense of rightness.

His cheek came down next to hers. He pulled back his hips, slowly pushed forward, pulled back, pushed forward. Every movement was controlled and deeply, deeply arousing.

When Shaye began to fear that she'd reach her limit before him, she unlocked her ankles and moved her thighs against his hips. Unable to resist, Noah ran his palms the length of her legs. The feel of the smooth, firm silk was too much. He made a low, throaty sound and within seconds surged into a throbbing climax. Only then did she allow herself the same release.

He whispered her name over and over until their bodies had begun to quieten. Then he framed her face with his hands and tipped it up. "I love you, Shaye." He sealed the vow with a long, sweet kiss, and when he held her back again, there were tears in her eyes. "There are more secrets. I know that. But I do love you. Secrets and all. I don't care where you've been or what you've done. I love you."

She didn't return the words, but held him in tight, trembling arms. *Do I love him? Can I love him? Will I be asking for trouble if I love him? I can't control him. I can't control myself when I'm with him. If love is forever, can it possibly work?*

THE ACTIVITY that followed offered Shaye a welcome escape from her thoughts. She and Noah dressed, ate a fast breakfast, then joined Victoria and Samson on deck. Though the rain had stopped, the sky remained heavily overcast. Ever the optimist, Samson said it was for the best, that without the sun, they'd be cooler.

Shaye wondered about that. It was hot and sticky anyway. One glance at Noah told her he felt the same, and she noted that Samson had even passed up his pirate outfit in favor of more practical shorts and T-shirt. He wore his tricorne, though. She couldn't begrudge him that.

Since there had, as yet, been no stars by which to measure their position, Samson was left with making a sight judgment. Having carefully studied the small bay from the deck of the sloop, he'd already decided that it compared favorably with the one on his map. When he questioned Noah and Shaye about what they'd seen when they'd been ashore the night before, they looked at each other sheepishly. He didn't pursue the issue.

Loading the dingy with shovels and a pick, they left the *Golden Echo* securely anchored and rowed to shore. As soon as they'd safely beached the raft, Samson pulled out his map.

"Okay, let's look for the rose."

Shaye winced. Noah sent her a wink that made her feel a little better. Then he, too, turned his attention to the map. "According to this, the rock should be near the center of the back of the lagoon and not too far from shore."

Samson nodded distractedly. His gaze alternated between the map and the beach before them. "That's what the map suggests, though I dare say it wasn't drawn to scale." He refolded and pocketed the fragile paper. "Let's take a look."

The spot where they were headed was a short distance along the beach. After allowing Samson and Victoria a comfortable lead, Noah took Shaye's hand and they set off.

"Excited?" he asked.

"Certainly."

He cast her a sidelong glance. "Is that a little dryness I detect in your tone?"

"Me? Dryness?"

"Mmm. Do you believe we'll find a treasure?"

"Of course we'll find a treasure," she said. Her eyes were on Samson's figure striding confidently ahead.

"Forget about my uncle. What do *you* think?"

"Honestly?" She paused. "I doubt it."

"Are you in a betting mood?"

"You think there is a treasure?"

"Honestly? I doubt it."

"Then why bet?"

"'Cause it's fun. You say no. I say yes. Whoever wins . . . whoever wins . . ."

She was smiling. "Go on. I want to know. What will you bet?"

"How about a pair of Mets tickets?"

"Boo-hiss."

"How about a weekend in the country?"

"Not bad." She pursed her lips. "What country?"

He chuckled. She'd deftly ruled out his place in Vermont. "Say Canada—the Gaspé Peninsula?"

"Getting warm."

"England—Cornwall?"

"Getting warmer."

"France?"

"A small château in Normandy?" At his nod, she grinned. "You're on."

He studied her upturned face. "You look happy. Feeling that confident you'll win?"

"No. But win or lose I get to visit Normandy."

He threw back his head with an exaggerated, "Ahh," and made no mention of the fact that according to the terms of the bet, win or lose, she'd be visiting Normandy with *him*. For a weekend? No way. It'd be a full week or two if he had his say.

Draping an arm around her shoulder, he held her to his side. Their hips bumped as they walked. She suspected he was purposely doing it and, in the spirit of fun, she bumped him right back. They were nearly into an all-out-kick-and-dodge match when Samson's applause cut into their play.

"Bravo! Nice footwork there, Shaye. Noah, your legs are too long. Better quit while you're ahead." Turning his back on them, he propped his hands on his hips and studied the shoreline. "This is our starting point."

"Quit while I'm ahead," Noah muttered under his breath as he looked around. There wasn't a rock in sight. He lowered his head toward Shaye's. "Seaweed, driftwood, sand and palm trees. That's it."

"Ahh, but beyond the palm trees—"

"More palm trees."

"And a wealth of other trees and shrubs—"

"And monkeys and parrots and alligators—"

"Alligators! Are you kidding?"

"Would I kid you about something like that?"

"Victoria," Shaye cried plaintively, "you didn't tell me there'd be alligators!"

"No problem, sweetheart," Victoria said breezily. "Just watch where you step."

Samson started toward the palms and gestured for them to follow. Within ten minutes it was clear that they were going to have to broaden the search. They'd seen quite a few rocks among the foliage, but nothing of significant size and nothing remotely resembling a rose.

"Let's fan out. Shaye, you and Noah head south. Victoria and I will head north. Don't go farther inland then we are now, and head back out to the beach in, say—" he checked his watch "—half an hour. Okay?"

"Okay," Shaye and Noah answered together. They stood watching as Samson and Victoria started off.

Noah raked damp spikes of hair from his forehead. "Man, it's warm in here."

"Do you want to take off your shirt?"

"And get bitten alive?" He swatted something by his ear. "Was there any insect repellent in the dingy?"

"I think Samson had some in his pocket."

"Lots of good it'll do us there," he grumbled, then did an about-face to study the area Samson had assigned them. "Wish we had a machete."

"It's not that dense." She took a quick breath. "Noah, wouldn't alligators prefer a wetter area?"

"There are marshes just a little bit inland." He was studying the jungle growth. "I think if we work back and forth diagonally we'll be able to cover the most space in the least time."

"Is it alligators that bite, or crocodiles?"

"Crocs, I think." He rubbed his hands together, clearly working up enthusiasm. "Okay. L-l-l-l-l-let's hit it!"

Shaye stayed slightly behind Noah on the assumption that he'd scare away anything crawling in their path. She kept a lookout on either side, more than once catching herself when her eyes skimmed right past a rock formation simply because it didn't have a scaly back, a long tail, four squat legs and an ominous snout.

They followed a zigzag pattern, working slowly from jungle to shore and back. Soon after the third shore turn, they stopped short.

"It is a large rock," Shaye said cautiously.

"Would you go so far as to call it a boulder?"

"Depends how you define boulder. But it does have odd markings. Do you think it resembles a rose?"

Noah tipped his head and, squinted. "With a stretch of the imagination."

"Mmm. Let's look around a little more."

They completed that zig and the next zag and found a number of rocks that could, by that same stretch of the imagination, be said to resemble a rose. None were as large, though, and none stood alone as the first had.

"That has to be it," Noah decided.

Against her better judgment, Shaye felt a glimmer of excitement. "Let's tell the others." They started back. When they cleared the palms, they saw Samson and Victoria heading their way.

"We found it!" Shaye cried.

Victoria stopped short. "*We* found it!"

"Oh boy," Noah murmured.

Samson beamed. It looked as though they had a double puzzle on their hands, which was going to make the adventure that much more exciting.

10

THE FOUR TREKKED from one rock to the other. "Either could be it," Victoria decided.

"Or neither," said Shaye.

Noah mopped his face on the sleeve of his T-shirt. "If you ask me, there are half a dozen other rocks here that could fit the bill." He received three dirty looks so quickly that he held up a hand. "Okay. Okay. I'll admit that these two are more distinctive than the others." He frowned at the rock. "What do you think, Samson—could the markings be man-made?"

"They could be, but I don't think they are. Even allowing for lousy artistry and the effects of time, something man-made would be more exact. These are just irregular enough to look authentic."

"Which leaves the major problem of choosing between the two rocks," Shaye reminded them. "Does the map give any clue?"

Samson removed the map from his shirt pocket and extended it to her. She unfolded it and studied it. Victoria peered in from her right side, Noah hung over her left shoulder.

After a short time, Shaye and Victoria looked at each other in dismay. "You were right before," Victoria told Noah. "According to the map, the rose is smack in the middle of the back stretch of beach. But there wasn't any rose-shaped rock there. It has to be one of these two."

"But which one?" Shaye asked.

"Which looks more like a rose?"

"I don't know, so we're back to square one."

Victoria held up a finger. "I want to look at the other rock." Grabbing Shaye's arm, she propelled her through the jungle to the second rock.

Samson and Noah didn't move. They waited until the women returned, then Noah asked, "Okay, ladies, which rock will it be?"

"This one—"

"That one—"

He dug into his shorts pocket. "I'll flip a coin."

"You can't flip a coin on something as crucial," Victoria cried.

Shaye agreed.

"I don't have a coin anyway," Noah said and turned to Samson. "Got a coin?"

Samson produced a jackknife. "We'll let it fall. The slant of the handle will determine which rock we go with."

"A jackknife—"

"Is worse than a coin!"

The women were overruled. Samson flipped the knife. They went with the southern rock, the one Shaye and Noah had found and, coincidentally, the one Shaye thought looked more like a rose.

Putting defeat behind her, Victoria read off instructions from the map. "Seventeen paces due west."

"How long is a 'pace'?" Shaye asked.

"An average stride. Noah, you walk it off."

"Noah's stride can't be average. Samson, you walk it off."

"Samson is nearly as tall as Noah," Victoria pointed out. "Shaye you do it. Just stretch your stride a little."

With the others supervising, Shaye accepted and consulted the compass, marked off fifteen paces due west, then stopped.

"You need two more," Noah said.

"Two more paces will take me into the middle of that bromeliad colony. What do the instructions say from there, Victoria?"

"Twenty paces due south."

"Twenty paces due south," Shaye murmured, making estimates as she positioned herself on the south side of the bromeliads. "Say we're two paces south now. Three... four... five..."

Her progress was broken from time to time by another bit of the forest that was impenetrable, but she finally managed to reach twenty. Victoria, Samson and Noah were by her side.

"What now?" she asked.

"Southeast twenty-one paces," Victoria read.

"This is really pretty inexact—"

"Twenty-one paces," Noah coaxed. "Walk 'em off."

Compass in hand, she started walking. Victoria counted, while Samson followed the progress with an indulgent smile on his face. In the same manner they worked their way through additional twists and turns.

"What next?" Shaye finally asked.

"Nothing," Victoria said. "That's it. A big X on the map. You're standing on the treasure."

Shaye looked at the hard-packed sand beneath her feet. "It could be here, or here." She pointed three feet to the right. "Or even over there. Now, if we had some kind of metal detector, we might be in business."

"No metal detector," Samson said. "That would be cheating."

"But treasure hunters always use metal detectors," Shaye argued.

"We don't have one," Noah said in a tone that settled the matter. If there was no metal detector, there was no metal detector.

Shaye pointed straight down and raised skeptical eyes to Noah, who gave a firm nod.

A quick trip to the dingy produced the digging equipment and a knapsack that Victoria had filled with sandwiches and cans of soda earlier that morning. The soda had gone a little warm, but none of them complained. It was thirst quenching. The sandwiches were energizing. The insect repellent was better late than never.

They started digging in pairs, trading off every few minutes. There were diversions—a trio of spider monkeys swinging through the nearby trees, the chatter of a distant parrot—and the occasional reward of a quick swim in the bay. But by three in the afternoon, they had a large, deep hole and no treasure.

They'd initially dug down three feet, then another, then had widened the hole until it was nearly five feet in diameter. Now Noah stood at its center with his arms propped on the shovel handle. He looked hot and tired.

Shaye, who'd stopped digging several minutes before, sat on the edge of the hole. Victoria was beside her, and Samson stood behind them with a pensive look on his face.

"How much deeper do we go before we give up?" Shaye asked softly. She felt every bit as hot and tired as Noah looked.

"It has to be here," Victoria said. "Maybe we marked it out wrong."

"It *doesn't* have to be here," Shaye reminded her. "We knew there was the possibility the map was a sham."

Noah leaned against their side of the pit. He pushed his hair back with his forearm, smudging grime with the sweat. "I've dug the pick in another foot and hit nothing. I doubt a pirate would have buried anything deeper than this."

"If only we knew what we were looking for," Victoria mused. "Large box, small box, tiny leather pouch . . ."

Shaye sighed. "It's like trying to find a needle in a haystack, and you don't even know which haystack to look in."

"The other rock," said Noah. "It has to be that. We picked the wrong one to start pacing from." He hoisted himself from the hole. "Y'know, whoever drew up this map was either a jokester, a romantic or an imbecile."

Shaye was right beside him, followed by Victoria and Samson, as he strode quickly toward the other rock. "What do you mean?"

"The directions. They were given in paces west, south, southeast, etc., when we would have reached the same spot by one set of paces heading due south. When I first saw the map, I assumed there were natural barriers to go around, but we didn't find any." He'd reached the second rock and was studying the map. Then he closed his eyes and made some mathematical calculations.

"How many paces due south?" Samson asked.

"Let's try sixty-five."

He stood back while Shaye marked sixty-five paces due south. When she finished counting, she was standing directly before the first rock. She looked up at the others.

Victoria was the only one who seemed to share her surprise. "Let's walk it off the original way," she suggested.

So Shaye went back, walked through the directions again, and wound up in the same spot, directly before the second rock. "He was a jokester," she decided in dismay.

Samson scratched the back of his head. "He has made things interesting."

"Interesting?" Victoria echoed, then grinned. "Mmm, I suppose he's done that." She shifted her gaze from Samson to Noah, who was striding off. "Where are you going?"

"To get the shovels."

"We're not going to do this now, are we?"

"Why not?"

Shaye ran after him, looping her elbow through his when she caught up. "Isn't it a little late in the day to start something new?"

"It's only four."

"But we've been digging all day."

"All afternoon," he corrected.

"The treasure's not going anywhere."

His eyes twinkled. "I'm curious to see if it's there."

"But wouldn't it be smarter to start again fresh tomorrow morning?"

Having arrived back at the first hole, he scooped up the pick and shovels. Then he leaned in close to Shaye and whispered, "But if we finish this up tonight, we can do whatever we want tomorrow."

She took in a shaky breath and whispered back, "But aren't you tired?"

"Are you?"

"Yes. And it looks like it might rain any minute."

"Then we'll have to work quickly," he said with a mischievous grin and started back toward the rock.

As it happened, Noah did most of the work. Shaye made a show of assisting, silently reasoning that she was young and strong. But the digging she'd done earlier had taken its toll. She was tired. She had blisters. To make matters worse, the hole was only three feet deep and wide when it started to drizzle.

"Leave it," Shaye urged.

Samson agreed. "She's right, Noah. We can finish in the morning."

"No way," he grunted, setting to work with greater determination. "Another eighteen inches either way." He hoisted a shovelful of wet sand and tossed it aside with another grunt. "That's all we need."

"We can do it tomorrow—"

"And have the rain wash the sand—" another toss, another grunt "—back into this hole during the night? Just a little more now—give me forty-five minutes." Another shovelful hit the pile. "If I haven't struck anything by then, I'll quit."

The rain grew heavier. When Shaye eased into the hole and started to shovel again, Noah set her bodily back up on the edge. Likewise, when Samson tried to give a hand, Noah insisted that he could work more freely on his own.

They were all soaked, but no one complained. The rain offered relief from the heat. Unfortunately, though, it made Noah's work harder. Each shovelful of sand was wetter and heavier than the one before, and, if anything, he seemed bent on making this hole bigger than the last. He was obviously tiring. And neither the shovel nor the pick, which he periodically used, were turning up anything remotely resembling hidden treasure.

Then it happened. Shaye was watching Noah work under the edge of the large rock, wondering what would happen if the rain lessened the stability of the sand, when suddenly that side of the hole began to crumble.

"Noah!" she cried, but the rock was already sliding. Through eyes wide with horror, she saw Noah twist to the side and try to scramble away without success. He gave a deep cry of pain as the lower half of his right leg was pinned beneath the rock. In a second, Shaye had shimmied down into the narrow space left and was pushing against the rock, as were Samson and Victoria from above.

It wouldn't budge.

"Oh God," Shaye whispered. She took a quick look at Noah's ashen face and pushed harder, but the rock had sunk snugly in the hole with precious little space for maneuvering.

Samson, too, was pale, but he kept calm. "Let me take your place, Shaye. You and Victoria scoot up against the side, put your feet flat against the rock and push as hard as you can when I say so."

They hurried into position. He gave the word. They pushed. Nothing happened.

"Again," he ordered. "Now!"

Nothing happened that time or, when they'd slightly altered position, the next. Even Noah tried then, though he wasn't at the best angle—or in the best condition—to help. Despite the varied attempts they made, the rock didn't move.

Samson shook his head. "We can't get leverage. If we could only raise it the tiniest bit, even for a few seconds, you could pull free. A broom handle would snap. We could try a palm—"

Noah gave a rough shake of his head and muttered, "Too thick."

"Not at the top, but it's too weak there. We need metal."

"We don't have metal," Noah said tightly. The lower part of his leg was numb, but pain was shooting through his thigh. In an attempt to ease the pressure, he turned and sank sideways on the sand.

Shaye's heart was pounding. She couldn't take her eyes off him. "There has to be something on the *Golden Echo* we can use," she said frantically, then tacked on an even more frantic, "isn't there?"

Noah groped for her hand, but it was Samson to whom he spoke. "There's nothing on the boat. You'll have to go for help."

Samson had reached the same conclusion and was already on his feet and motioning for Victoria. "We'll make a quick trip to the boat for supplies. You'll stay here, Shaye?"

"Yes!"

With a nod, he was gone.

Shaye turned back to Noah. He was resting his head against the side of the hole. She combed the wet hair from his forehead. "How do you feel?"

He was breathing heavily. "Not great."

"Think it's broken?"

"Yup."

"I should have seen it coming. I should have been able to warn you."

"My fault. I was careless. Too tired." The word broke into a gasp. "I usually do better—"

She put a finger to his lips. "Shh. Save your strength."

He grabbed her hand. "Stay close."

She slid into the narrow space facing him and tucked his hand beneath her chin. For a long time neither of them spoke. The rain continued to fall. Noah closed his eyes against the pain that he could feel more clearly now below his knee.

Shaye alternately watched him and the shore. "Where are they?" she demanded finally in a tight, panicky whisper.

Noah didn't answer. It was fast getting dark. The rain continued to fall.

Samson and Victoria returned at last with a replenished knapsack, rain ponchos and two lanterns. Then Samson knelt with a hand on Noah's shoulder. "We'll be back as soon as we can. There are painkillers in the sack. Don't be a hero, and whatever you do, don't try to tug that leg free now or you'll make the damage worse."

Noah, who'd already figured that out, simply nodded.

"Hurry," Shaye whispered, hugging both Victoria and Samson before they left. "Hurry." Moments later, she watched them push off in the dingy, then she sank down beside Noah and put her hand to his cheek. "Can I get you anything?"

He shook his head.

"Food?"

Again he shook his head.

"Drink?"

"Later."

She didn't bother to ask if he wanted the poncho. She knew that he wouldn't. In spite of the rain, the night was warm. It did occur to her, though, that they'd feel more comfortable if they were leaning against rubber rather than grit. Popping up, she spread the ponchos over the side of the hole. Noah shifted and helped, then sank back against them with his head tipped up to the rain. Very gently, she washed the lingering grime from his face with her fingers, then slid back to his side and watched him silently.

His facial muscles twitched, then rested. His brow furrowed, then relaxed. Then he swore under his breath.

"The leg?"

"God, it hurts."

"Damn the rose. I had a feeling. I knew it would be bad luck."

"No. My own stupid fault. I was so determined to dig, so determined to find that treasure."

"It was the bet—"

"Uh-uh. I just wanted to get it done. But I should have anticipated the problem. Take the ground out from under a rock and it's gonna fall."

"You didn't take much out. I had to have been the rain."

"I should have seen it coming."

"*I* should have. I was the one sitting there watching. If I'd been able to give you a few more seconds' warning..."

Noah curved his hand around the back of her neck and brought her face to his throat. "Not your fault." He kissed her temple and left his mouth there. "I'm glad you're with me."

She lifted her face and kissed him. "I just wish there were something I could do to make you more comfortable."

"How about...that drink..."

She quickly dug into the knapsack, extracted first a can of Coke, then, more satisfactorily, a bottle of wine. Tugging out the cork, she handed it to him. "Want a sandwich with it?"

He tipped the bottle and took several healthy swallows. "And dilute the effects? No way?"

"You want to get smashing drunk?"

He took another drink. "Not smashing. Just mildly." He closed his eyes again, and the expression of pain that crossed his face tore right through Shaye.

"Is it getting worse?" she whispered fearfully.

He said nothing for a minute, but seemed to be gritting his teeth. Then he took a shaky breath and opened his eyes. "Talk to me."

"About what?"

"You."

"Me? There's nothing much to say—"

"I want to hear about the past. I want to hear about all the things you've sidestepped before."

"I haven't—"

"You have."

She searched his eyes, seeing things that went beyond the physical pain he was experiencing. "Why does it matter?"

"Because I love you."

She put her fingertips to his mouth, caressing his lips moments before she leaned forward and kissed them. "I didn't expect you in my life, Noah," she breathed brokenly, then kissed him again.

"Tell me what you feel."

"Frightened. Confused." She sought out his lips again, craving their drugging effect.

He gave himself up to her kiss, but as soon as it ended, the pain was back. "Talk to me."

She carried his hand to her mouth and kissed his knuckles.

"My leg hurts like hell, Shaye. If you want to help, you can give me something to think about beside the fact that it's probably broken in at least three places."

"Don't say that—"

"Not to mention scraped raw."

"Noah—"

"I may well be lame for life."

"Don't even think that!"

"Tell me you wouldn't care."

"If you were lame? Of course, I'd care! The thought of your being in pain—"

"Tell me that you wouldn't care if I were lame, that you'd love me anyway."

"I'd love you if *both* legs were lame! What a stupid thing to ask."

"Not stupid," he said quietly, soberly, almost grimly. "Not stupid at all. Do you love me, Shaye?"

Shocked, she looked at him.

"Do you?" he prodded.

She bit her lip. "Yes."

"You haven't thought about it before now?"

"I've tried not to."

"But you do love me?"

She frowned. "If loving a person means that you like him even when you hate him, that you think about him all the time, that you hurt when he's hurt—" she took a tremulous breath "—the answer is yes."

"Ahh, baby," he said with a groan that held equal parts relief and pain. He drew her in close and held her as tightly as his awkward sideways position would allow.

"I love you," she whispered against his chest, "do love you."

His arms tightened. He winced, then groaned, then mumbled, "Talk to me. Talk to me, Shaye. Please?"

There seemed no point in holding back. With the confession he'd drawn from her, Noah had broken down the last of her defenses. He knew her. He knew what made her tick. He knew what pleased her, hurt her, drove her wild. Revealing the details of her past to him was little more than a formality.

Closing her eyes, Shaye began to talk. She told him about her childhood and the teenage years when she'd grown progressively wild. She told him about going off to college, about being free and irresponsible and believing that she had the world on a string. She told him about the boys and the men, the trips, the adventures, the apartments and the garret. Once started, she spilled it all. She wanted Noah to know everything.

For the most part, he listened quietly. Once or twice he made ceremony of wiping the rain from his face, but she suspected he was covering up a wince. At those times she stopped, offered him aspirin, and finally plied him with more wine, which was all the painkilling he'd accept. And she went on talking.

Only when she was near the end did she falter. She grew still, eyes downcast, hands tightly clenched.

"What happened then?" he prodded in a voice weakened by pain. "You were with André when you got a call from Shannon, and . . . ?"

She raked her teeth over her lower lip.

"Shaye?"

She took a broken breath. "She was in trouble. She'd been hanging around a pal of André's named Geoff, and when he introduced her to another guy, a friend of his, she didn't think anything of it. The friend turned out to be from the vice squad. Poor Shannon. She was nineteen at the time, not nearly sophisticated enough to protect herself from the Geoffs of the world. He was picked up on a dozen charges. She was arrested for possession of cocaine. She never knew what hit her."

"And you blamed yourself."

"I was at fault. I'd introduced her to André, André had introduced her to Geoff. I should have checked Geoff out myself." She waved a hand impatiently. "But it was more than that. The whole *scene* was wrong. Rebellion for the sake of rebellion, adventure of the sake of adventure, sex for the sake of sex—very little that went deeper, and nothing at all that resulted in personal growth. For six years I did that." She was shaking all over. "Blame myself? Not only was I responsible for what happened to Shannon, by rights, I should have been the one arrested!"

"Shh," Noah whispered against her temple. "It's okay."

"It's not!"

"What finally happened to Shannon?"

Shaye took several quick breaths to calm herself. "Victoria came to the rescue. She introduced us to a lawyer friend who introduced us to another lawyer friend, and between the two of them, Shannon got off with a suspended sentence and probation. She went on for a degree in communications and has a terrific job now in Hartford."

He shifted, and swallowed down a moan. The pain in his leg was excruciating. He had to keep his mind off it. "Sounds like she got off lighter than you did," he said tightly.

"Lighter?"

"You sentenced yourself to a lifetime of hard labor."

"No. I just decided to become very sane and sensible."

"Where do I fit into sane and sensible?"

She smoothed wet hair back from her forehead with the flat of her hand. "I don't know."

"Do you see me as being sane and sensible?"

"In some respects, yes. In others, no."

"And the 'no's' frighten you."

She nodded.

"Why?"

"Because I can't control them. Because you can be spontaneous and impulsive and irreverent, and that's everything I once was that nearly ended tragically!"

"But you like it when I'm that way. That's part of the attraction."

"I know," she wailed.

"And it's not bad. Look at it rationally, Shaye. You're nearly thirty now. Your entire outlook on life has matured since the days when you were wild." He caught in a breath, squeezed his eyes shut, finally went on in a raspy voice. "But you haven't found a man to love because the men you allow yourself to see don't excite you. You'd never have allowed yourself to see me if we'd met back in civilization, would you?"

"No."

"But there's nothing wrong with what we share! Okay, so we go nuts together in bed. Is that harmful? If it's just the two of us, and we're consenting adults, and we get up in the morning perfectly sane and sensible. Where's the harm?" His voice had risen steadily in pitch, and he was breathing raggedly by the time he finished.

"Oh God, Noah," she whispered. "What can I do—"

"Talk. Just talk."

She did, trying her best to tune out his pain. "I hear what you're saying. It makes perfect sense. But then I get to worrying and even the sensible seems precarious."

"You trust me?"

"I . . . yes."

"And love me?"

She nodded.

"Nothing is precarious. I'll protect you."

"But I have to be responsible, myself. That was one of the first things I learned from Shannon's fiasco."

"Ahh, Shaye, Shaye . . ." He tightened his arm around her shoulder and pressed his cheek to her wet hair. "You've gone to extremes. You don't have to be on guard every minute. There are times to let go and times not to." He stopped, garnering his strength. "Where's the lightness in your life, the sunshine, the frivolity? We all need that sometimes. Not all the time, just sometimes. There has to be a balance—don't you see?" His words had grown more and more strained. He loosened his hold on her and took a long drink of wine.

Shaye looked up, eyes wide. She stroked the side of his face with the backs of her fingers. "Don't talk so much, Noah. Please. It must be taking something out of you."

"It's the only thing that's helping. No, that's not true. The wine helps. And you. Your being here. Marry me, Shaye. I want you to marry me."

"I—"

"It looks like the trip is going to be cut short. We have to face the future."

"But—"

"I love you, Shaye. I didn't plan to fall in love. I've never really been in love before in my life. But I do love you."

"But these are such . . . bizarre circumstances. How can you possibly know what your feelings will be back in the real world?"

"I know my feelings," he said with a burst of strength. "I know what's been wrong with my life, what's been missing in the women I've known. You have everything I want. You're dignified and poised and intelligent. You're witty and gentle. You're compassionate and loyal. You're gorgeous. And you're spectacular in my arms. I meant it when I said I wanted you to mother my children. I do want that, Shaye. But I want you first and foremost for *me*." He punctuated the last with a loud, involuntary groan, followed by a pithy oath.

Shaye was on her knees in a minute, cradling his dripping face with both hands. "Let me get the codeine."

He shook his head. "Wine." He lifted the bottle and swallowed as much as he could.

"Where are they?" she cried, looking out to sea.

"They've just left. Won't be back until morning."

"Morning! Why morning?"

"It's a lee coast. We lucked out yesterday. It'll take them a while to reach Limón—"

"Isn't Moin closer?"

"No resources. Samson may try it, but by the time he locates a rescue team—"

"He has to do something before morning. You're in pain."

"Make that agony."

"This is no time for joking, Noah."

"I'm not."

"Oh. Oh God, isn't there anything I can do?"

"Say you'll marry me."

"I'll marry you."

"Ahh. Feels better already." He pried his head from the poncho. "Is there another bottle of wine?"

She reached for the bottle he held and saw that it was nearly empty. With relief, she found two more bottles in the knapsack. Opening one, she gave it to Noah in exchange for the first, the contents of which she proceeded to indulge in herself.

Had she just agreed to marry Noah?

She took another drink.

He drew her against his chest and encircled her with his arms, leaving the wine bottle to dangle against her side. "I need to hold on," he said, his voice husky with pain.

"Hold on," she whispered. "Hold on."

They sat like that for a while. Shaye heard the rain and the lap of the sea on the shore, but mostly she heard Noah's heart, beating erratically beneath her ear.

"I'm well-respected in the community," he muttered out of the blue. "I give to charity. I pay my taxes. Okay, so I do the unexpected from time to time, but I've never done anything illegal or immoral."

Gently, soothingly, she stroked his ribs, working at the tension in the surrounding muscles.

"I'll buy us a place midway between Manhattan and Philly, so you won't have to leave your job."

She kissed his collarbone.

"In fact," he rushed on, "you don't have to work at all if you don't want to. I'm loaded."

She laughed.

"I am," he protested.

"I believe you," she said, still smiling, thinking how incredibly much she did love him.

He took a shuddering breath, then another drink of wine. "I want the whole thing—the house, the kids, the dog, the station wagon."

"You do?"

"Don't you?"

"Yes, but I didn't think you would."

"Too conventional?"

"No, no. Very stable."

He closed a fist around her ponytail, pressed her head to his throat and moaned, "This isn't how it was supposed to be. There's nothing romantic in this. It's *sick*. My damn leg's caught under a rock. I can't move. I can't sweep you off your feet and carry you to bed, or bend you back over my arm and kiss you senseless. I'm not sure I can even get it up—that's how much everything down there hurts!"

Shaye knew he was in severe pain. She knew he was feeling frustrated. She couldn't do anything about either, so she decided to use humor. "The Playboy of the Pampas—impotent?"

"Not impotent—temporarily sidelined. You'll still marry me, won't you?"

"I'll still marry you." She took a deep breath and looked around. "It is a waste, though. We did so well in the rain last night, just think of what we could have done tonight." She moved her lips against his jaw, her voice an intimate whisper. "I'd like to make love in the water. Not deep water—shallow, just a few feet out from shore. Do you remember how it was when we were swimming? Only this time neither of us would have suits on, and there'd be a sandy floor for maneuvering, but the tide would wash around us. I'd wrap my legs around you—"

Noah interrupted her with a feral growl. "Enough. You've made your point."

"I have?"

He tried to shift to a more comfortable position, which was nearly impossible, given the circumstances.

Shaye felt instantly contrite. "Can I help?" she whispered, dropping her hand to his swollen sex.

He covered it and pressed it close for a minute, then raised it to his chest. "I think I'll take a rain check."

He took another drink, then held the bottle to her lips while she did the same. The sounds of the rain and the sea and the jungle night surrounded them, and for a time they sat in silence. Then Shaye asked, "The lanterns will keep the alligators away, won't they?"

He nodded.

"Hungry?"

He shook his head.

"Is there any chance of this hole flooding?"

He shook his head again.

"Do you have Blue Cross-Blue Shield?"

"Through the nose." A little while later, he said, "Maybe you're pregnant."

"No."

"Are you taking the pill?"

"No. But my period just ended. Last night was about as safe a time as any could be."

He considered that, then said, "No wonder you felt so lousy at the start of the trip."

She snorted. "You should have seen me when we first got to the hotel in Barranquilla."

"Don't use anything."

"What?"

"When we make love. I like knowing that there's a chance . . ."

"You really do want children."

"Very much. If you want to wait, though. I'll understand."

But the more she thought about it, the more Shaye liked the idea of growing big with Noah's child. She smiled into the night.

"You are going to marry me, aren't you?" he asked.

"I've said I would."

"What if you change your mind?"

"I won't."

"What if you have second thoughts when we get back home?"

"I won't."

"Why not?"

"I can't answer that now. Ask me again later."

He did, several times during the course of the night, but it wasn't until a pair of helicopters closed noisily in on the beach the following morning that Shaye had an answer for him.

She'd been with Noah throughout the night, had suffered with him and worried for him, had done what little she could to make him comfortable. She'd forced him to eat half a sandwich for the sake of his strength and had limited her own intake of wine to leave more for him. She'd sponged him off when the rain stopped and the air grew thick and heavy. She'd batted mosquitoes from his skin and had held his hand tightly when he'd twisted in pain.

The night had been hell. She never wanted to live through another like it. But she knew she wouldn't have been anywhere else in the world that night, and that was what she told Noah when the sheer relief of his impending rescue loosened her thoughts.

"You have the ability to make me happy, sad, excited, frustrated, angry, aroused and confused—but through it all I feel incredibly alive."

She combed her fingers through his hair. "You have the spirit and the sense of adventure I had before, only you've channeled it right." Affectionately she brushed some sand off his neck. "I want you to help me do that. Make my life full. Be my friend and protector." She kissed his forehead. "And lover. I want all that and more." She shot a glance at the crew bounding from the chopper, then tacked on, "Think you can handle it?"

He was a mess—dirty, sweaty, with one leg crushed beneath a boulder—but the look he sent her was eloquent in promise and love. She knew that she'd never, never forget it.

Epilogue

"Two helicopters?" Deirdre asked.

Victoria nodded. "One for the medics, the other for the fellows who raised the rock."

Leah winced. "Noah must have been out of his mind with pain by that time."

"He was out of it with something—whether pain or wine, I'll never know. The doctors in Limón did a preliminary patch-up job while Samson arranged for our transportation home. Noah's had surgery twice in the six weeks we've been back. He's scheduled to go in for a final procedure next week."

"Is the prognosis good?"

"Excellent, thank God. But even if it weren't, Noah's a fighter." She sighed. "He's quite a man."

Deirdre curled her legs beneath her on the chaise. It was the last day in August, a rare cool, dry, sunny summer day in New York, and Victoria's rooftop garden was the place to be. "When did they get married?"

Victoria smiled. "Four days after we got back. It was beautiful. Very simple. A judge, their closest friends and relatives." Her eyes grew misty. "Shaye was radiant. I know they say that about all brides, but she was. She positively glowed. And when Noah...presented her with...that single rose..."

Leah handed her a tissue, which Victoria waved around, as though it didn't occur to her to wipe her tears.

"When he gave her the rose, he said...he said—" her voice dropped to a tremulous whisper "—so softly and gently that I wouldn't have heard if I hadn't been standing right there..."

Both women were waiting wide-eyed. Deirdre leaned forward and asked urgently, "What did he say?"

Victoria sniffled. "He said, 'One rose. Just one. Pure, fresh and new. And it's in our hands.'" She took in a shuddering breath. "It was so . . . beautiful . . ." She pressed the tissue to her trembling lip.

Leah didn't understand the deeper significance of Noah's words any more than Deirdre did, but the romance of it was still there. She sighed loudly, then burst into a helpless smile. "Victoria Lesser strikes again." She was delighted with Victoria's latest story. She'd had no idea what to expect when Victoria had invited her down for a visit, and now she couldn't wait to get back to tell Garrick. But there was still more she wanted to know. "What about you and Samson?"

Victoria took a minute to collect herself. "Yes?"

"I thought you liked him. You said that in spite of the accident the trip was wonderful."

"It was."

"Well?" Deirdre prompted. "Is that all you have to say— just that it was wonderful? Neil will spend the entire night cross-examining me if I don't have anything better to give him when I get home."

Gracefully pushing herself from her chair, Victoria breezed across the garden to pluck a dried petal from a hanging begonia. "It'd serve you right," she said airily, "after what the four of you did."

"It was poetic justice," Deirdre argued.

Leah agreed. "Just deserts."

"A taste of your own medicine."

"*Lex talionis.*" When Victoria turned to arch a brow her way, Leah translated. "The law of retribution. But all with the best of intentions." She paused. "So. Were our good intentions in vain?"

Victoria hesitated for a long moment. Her gaze skipped from Leah's face to Deirdre's. Then she slanted them both a mischievous grin. "I won't remarry, you know."

"We know," Deirdre said.

"He was . . . very nice."

Leah held her breath. "And . . . ?"

"And we've decided to make a return visit to Costa Rica next summer to find out for sure whether that treasure does exist. Noah and Shaye weren't thrilled with that thought; they're hung up on the idea of going to some château in Normandy. So we'll just have to put together another group. In the meantime, Samson thought he'd do a bicycle tour of the Rhineland and asked if I'd like to go along."

"Where does he get the time?" Deirdre asked. "I thought he taught."

"Vacations, sweetheart. Vacations." Her eyes twinkled and her cheeks grew pink. "And weekends. There are lovely things that can be done on weekends." Turning her back on the two younger women, she busied herself hand pruning a small dogwood. "I was thinking that I'd drive north next month. The foliage is beautiful when it turns. Samson has invited me to stay with him in Hanover, claims he makes a mean apple cider. Now, theoretically, making apple cider should be as boring as sin. But then, theoretically, Latin professors should be as boring as sin, too, and Samson isn't. I guess I'll have to give his apple cider a shot. . . ."